Miren Agur Meabe (Leke: and Basque philology. She Basque school in Bilbao ai years. She writes literature fr and prose. Her prizes include the 2001 and 2011 Critic's Poetry Awards for *Azalaren kodea* and *Bitsa eskuetan*, and the 2002, 2006, and 2011 Euskadi Prizes for her three young adult novels, *Itsaslabarreko etxea, Urtebete itsasargian,* and *Errepidea.* Her book *Mila magnolia-lore* is on the 2012 International Board on Books Honour's List. Some of the honorary awards she has received are the Lauaxeta Prize (2007), the Rosalia de Castro Prize (2012) and the Deia-Hemendik Prize (2015). Her writings have been translated into several languages, and into Braille. She has been a member of the Basque Academy of Letters since 2006.

Amaia Gabantxo is a writer, a flamenco singer and literary translator specialising in Basque literature. She currently teaches creative writing at the University of Chicago, and performs regularly in venues all over the city. As a translator of Basque literature she has received multiple awards for her work—lately, the OMI Writers Translation Lab award and a Mellon Fellowship for Arts and Scholarship, as well as a year-long artist's residency at the Instituto Cervantes of Chicago. Her latest literary translations include *Twist* by Harkaitz Cano for Archipelago Books in New York, and *Rock & Core* and *Downhill* by poet Gabriel Aresti for the University of Nevada Press. She's writing a novel in flamenco form.

A GLASS EYE

*Translated from Basque
by Amaia Gabantoxo*

Miren Agur Meabe

PARTHIAN

Parthian, Cardigan SA43 1ED
www.parthianbooks.com
A Glass Eye first published as *Kristalezko begi bat* in 2013 (Susa)
First published in 2018
© Miren Agur Meabe 2018
© This translation by Amaia Gabantxo 2018
ISBN 978-1-912109-54-8
Editor: Susie Wild
Cover design by RJPHA
Typeset by Elaine Sharples
Printed in EU by Pulsio SARL
Published with the financial support of the Welsh Books Council,
Etxepare Institutoa Translation Grant,
and OMI Writers Translator Lab Award
British Library Cataloguing in Publication Data
A cataloguing record for this book is available from the British Library.

To my girlfriends.

And to M. Because of us.

'The eye is not a miner, says Virginia Woolf, not a diver, not a seeker after buried treasure. The eye floats us smoothly down a stream.' – **Marguerite Yourcenar**

'To be able to say how much love, is love but little.' – **Petrarch**

'But what if we are all fictioneers? What if we all continually make up the stories of our lives? […] Our life-stories are ours to construct as we wish, within or even against the constraints imposed by the real world…' – **J.M. Coetzee**

INTRODUCTION

I lost an eye, the left one, when I was thirteen.

My mother died in three-and-a-half months, due to ovarian cancer, when I was thirty-eight.

A few years ago I divorced. It would be beautiful to boast that my husband's gradual distancing was literature's fault, that it is well known that men, in general, don't like women who write books. That's what Marguerite Duras says in *Écrire*. But no: my husband loved me for many years, and I him, and we were for each other. Despite that, at some point we started not getting what we expected from one another, and that right there became the undertow of our existence. And, yes, that other love, the love of writing, came between us then.

Soon after our ship sunk, I had an adventure. I sought the shelter of a lover's embrace because a mammography revealed two shadows and because the eagerness this man showed for me (at the beginning I mistook it for love) made me feel special. I was egged on by a desire to soothe my fear, a hopelessness that sought to sweeten my despair, an urgency to channel my fury, a need to break rules, and by my dreams, because I often fall in love with my dreams. I am thirsty for: I am thirsty for butterflies, I don't know if what I mean can be understood. For now, the shadows in my breast are still. The relationship with that man didn't move forward either.

Soon, within a year, I handed in my resignation at work. It wasn't my place anymore. I am a full-time writer for the first time. I make a living as a writer-for-hire.

In any case, this past summer I forced myself to make a decision: I left M. Now I am struggling with the consequences. Sometimes I'm amazed that I can live quite a normal life still.

Other than that, I lost umbrellas, bus passes, bankcards, keys, shawls, earrings…

I haven't lost any friends though; at least none that I know.

I am forty-eight and like most people I have faced many losses. That is why I started to write this text. I think that writing in the first person will stop time from eating away all of my memories. So I am writing for myself, but for you too perhaps, because maybe you too are someone who has been beaten but not defeated by love.

THE PRICE OF MY PEARL

My left eye is made of glass. They gave it to me so that my sick eye wouldn't infect the healthy one, to avoid what they call sympathetic ophthalmia. When they told me that they had to remove my eye I was terrified: it's not an easy exercise to put aside something you've always had and to imagine your face with a fake eye on it, like a scream.

I couldn't erase two childhood images from my mind: the first one, of the gardener in the park and, the other, of an uncle from my father's side, because the glass eyes of those two men were exactly like targets, fixed, unmovable, dead. However, they explained to me that how the eye was lost (if by accident or by illness) and how neat the scar was after the extraction had an effect on the overall state and look of the eye socket.

Shotgun pellets took the gardener's eye out in a hunting accident; in my uncle's case it was a firecracker and a childhood friend's trick that did it. 'Look in the hole in that wall,' his friend said, 'there is a coin there, but I can't get at it... You try.' My uncle brought his eye close to the wall.

I lost mine to glaucoma. My eye became a twisted red marble. That deformity weighed heavily on my teenage years. Every now and then whispered words would reach me. 'Such a beautiful girl... it's a great pity.' Because of this, irony of ironies, I've always been much more despondent about the contours of my waist.

I kept my deteriorating eye until I finished my studies and started work in a Basque school. When I heard the nickname some students used for me I was very hurt, but what can you expect from cruel students.

Early on I had a doubt, an important one since I'm very emotional: whether it would be possible to cry without an eye. I cry easily. Tears are necessary to me, to prove to myself that I am a good person. At the same time, I also like that they provide transcendence to the events I experience. I find them a reliable measure.

The first time I wore my fake eye felt like walking out in the streets naked. But the shame, however, didn't last.

After weighing my existing preconceptions against the final result, I am pretty sure that I have been lucky with my pearl because, modern prostheses, being individualised, looks rather natural – unlike the old ones.

Be that as it may, when I get in the sack with a man for the first few times I am careful with the eye. Since I can't control the pressure in my eyelids at all (I don't like it, but my left eye is always half-open, even when I'm asleep), when I fuck I consciously try to control the eye and close it. Those who aren't used to it might find it disconcerting that my two eyes don't behave like identical twins all the time.

SAVE ME FROM ALL EVIL

I left M.

Since then, I sleep four or five hours at the most. I spend the better part of the night holding on to the edges of the mattress, arms spread crucifixion style. 'No, that isn't what the dead do,' I tell myself, 'the dead usually rest their hands on their laps.' I'm jealous of the dead.

Every so often I can't breathe. I imagine M.'s feet stepping on my breasts.

I need about half an hour to get dressed.

I zigzag around the room like a drunkard; I feel my way around it, hands on walls, as if the ground were about to give way.

The pain in my ribs awakes again (I have a cyst in my kidney that sometimes reminds me of its presence). It's obvious that, in me, goodbyes and sorrows plait into a single rope when it's time to cast something or someone off.

I haven't left the house other than for emergencies since July, only to run the odd errand or for brief visits to my oldies.

They've lent me a house in Les Landes. I arrived the day before yesterday. I have inhabited these landscapes before, on Easter holidays, with family. This time I come in secret, in early September, to escape my worries. 'I can't anymore,' I told the owners, a couple, friends of mine.

The villages here are all similar: the town square with its tiled fountain in the middle, the bakery, the tobacconist's, the glass-fronted bistro and the marble plaque on the side of the church:

Morts pour le patrie. It's only when you leave the centre that a few scattered houses appear, each with its own garden and surrounding pines.

Le Rayon Vert sits on top of a dune. You can hear the roar of the ocean, the rasp of a thousand seashells as they rub and tumble. There is a line of foam on the beach. Bulrush here and there, like silver hair. I found a dead seagull, belly up, eyes turned into yellow lentils. One of its legs was tangled in the metallic net that fences the car park off.

I had to shovel off a mound of sand blocking the front door. I scarcely had the energy to face such a task, but I did it, tears and whimpers notwithstanding. The wind is such in this corner of the world, sand gets in even through the keyholes. You need a shovel at hand, just like other places require you keep snow gloves or insect repellent nearby.

I switched the lights on and nibbled at the sandwich in my handbag while organising my bits.

I have come to write. But the pen in my hand feels like a pickaxe.

I will write, because writing down what I have to tell will give me some sort of sense of immortality (an otherwise ridiculous feeling, by the way). Once again, paper will save me from all evil. A page a day. That's what I promised myself.

I put my notebook, dictionary, watch, phone and cup of tea (a relaxing infusion of mint, lemon balm and lime blossom) on the table. I drink about half a dozen cups every day now; at night, Trazodone. Nothing soothes the pain.

THE VARIANTS OF PAIN

I never thought I would experience heartbreak so despondently again (or should I have known that I would?).

When pain is solid, it pulls you downward, like a flat stone that lives in your belly. Your head hangs low. Your weak neck muscles make it impossible to lift or turn it. When you try, if you're standing, you lose your balance. You feel like you bump into everything as you walk. You bring your hands to your belly then. You whimper, a choked sound devoid of hope, coming from an old animal, a puff of air born in the throat and blown through the nose.

Some other times the pain is sharp; a wire needling in between the ribs. That pain grabs your eyes and throat. It tends to bring tears, that pain, it awakens your self-pity. You wallow in words of despair until you drown in your predicament. When tears turn to hiccups you sit on the bed and remain still, looking at the ceiling, or at anything else in the room, a painting or a chair, until your breathing eases. You cover your face with your hands. You look like a woman in a Hopper painting then. (Harkaitz Cano is right when he says the old man is tired of being rattled in his grave every time we use him to legitimise our decadent, badly-understood melancholy. But oh well, I still find those women are my true reflection.)

Other times the pain is like a punch, if I unexpectedly bump into M., say at the fishmongers, the square or the pharmacy. Suddenly, everything moves very quickly, except him. The background becomes a blur I can barely see because the violence of the thumping in my temples won't let me look away from M.'s mouth. At times like that, when we exchange a couple of words and go our separate ways, my face hurts like I've been slapped.

The worst pain, however, is the claw pain. It scratches the walls of the intestine and they contract. You feel nauseous then, even if you haven't eaten anything in hours. You run to the bathroom and release bile and saliva. You want to think that in releasing that liquid you release a curse, that through vomit you let go of this undue punishment, because no man deserves such a grotesque display of sorrow. This is more than pain; it's agony.

This agony swallows me when I imagine M. with another woman. It could be a faceless someone, someone I don't know, a colleague from work, for example; or a woman from our village, a brunette or a blonde, a thin one; or a young girl, a shameless lass who enjoys telling tales of seducing older men to her friends. I see M. standing, pounding into her from behind. With every shove, the pendant I gave him (a green-grey stone the same colour as his eyes) dances a jig on his hairy chest. When this happens I grab the switch on the bedside lamp and I turn the light off, turn it on, turn it off again, turn it on again, and once again, turn off, turn on, off and on in a vain effort to erase that image.

I would prefer not to have a body. My body is a sack full of broken branches. I would be so much better off in a coffin. It is hard to imagine, unless you've experienced it, how heavy the burden of broken love can be.

LE RAYON VERT

I don't know why they gave the house this name.

The Green Ray is a book by Jules Verne, it's based on a real optic phenomena: when the sun hides behind a flat surface, its last rays refract onto the atmosphere in a range of amber-like colours. At the exact instant the sun disappears, the human eye can perceive a green ray.

According to legend, two people who see this ray at the same time will experience a bond of love. Perhaps the previous owners found this spot and thought it would be a good place for a house, in hopes they'd see the green ray. Or perhaps they saw the ray here, and that's why they built the house. Utter nonsense.

There is an Eric Rohmer film of that name too. It's been years since I saw it, but I found it a bit underwhelming.

The ground floor consists of one large room, one of those kitchen-lounges. The bathroom is downstairs too, and the junk room. The furniture is clean, no fingerprints in sight. Truly, how quickly we accept to drink from the glasses and sleep in the sheets strangers have just used, even if we hesitate at first, wondering if we'll find a dodgy stain or a curly pube. It's obvious that both the curtains and the eucalyptus branches behind the door have been hung only recently.

There are two rooms upstairs. I take the bigger one. The wood panels that run half way up the walls are painted white, like the rest of the room. The bed is against the window (too big, I say, as I caress my breasts). There is a wooden chest at the foot of the bed, a chimney in front, an armchair, and on the shelf, a ship in a bottle, *Souvenir des Landes*. A kilim rug breaks the monochromy.

It's warm, almost sweltering. I should remove the seagull before it starts to rot. The sun looks like the inner face of an oyster on the matt sky.

A GLASS EYE IS AN OBJECT

The first artificial eye in history is 4,800 years old. They found it in an archaeological site in the Burnt City, in what was ancient Mesopotamia, near the current frontier with Afghanistan. It was inside the head of a young woman, and was made of tar and animal fat. It has an iris at its centre, and gold rays imitating eye capillaries, less than half a millimetre thin.

It must have been hard for its owner to get used to that foreign object; I know that from experience. If a chickpea in the shoe hurts, a pebble in the eye socket is no nicer. Driven by pain, despair, or plain disappointment, many have taken hammer to eye to smash it.

But if you remove the prosthesis or lose it, scarring may take place, and this has consequences. In fact, it is not recommendable to take the eye out for long stretches, because the cavity tends to contract. In the worst of all cases, you might not be able to get it in again.

It gets harder and harder for me too, because of age. Not because my pulse is feeble, but because of the quality of my skin: the top eyelid is weaker, and as a result the eye's opening has narrowed; the lower lid has lost elasticity too (like all other parts of the body) and it barely bears the weight of the fake eye. This complicates the process of casting a new eye.

Truth is, the eye needs to be replaced every four or five years: the glass gets cloudy, like sea glass (tears are salty too). Taking into account how important eyes are in a person's face, experts recommend that the eye be replaced at those intervals: eyes that are used for too long tinge the expression with sadness (like overused feelings). Although they can't be classified as consumer products, glass eyes have a limited life expectancy.

And regarding the weakening of the skin, I should say that a couple of years ago, to stop the eye from falling out, they stitched the internal corner of my eyelid, like you would to take too-big trousers in at the waist. It was a quick repair. I remember the surgeon caressed my face as I lay waiting on the stretcher before we went into the operating room.

ABOUT THE EARTH AND THE AIR

I can't stay away from the phone. I leave it on the sink while I shower, on the bedside table when I go to bed. I never switch it off. I am always checking for messages. I get startled when one comes in because it might be from M. Then I get irritated because I have to admit that the sound of the ringtone flustered me.

In summer, crazy with insomnia, I would get up in the middle of the night and stumble on everything. Sometimes, I would grab a bottle and drink straight from it. Wearing nothing but a nightgown and very wild hair, like Lana Turner or Lee Remick in those old movies. The alcohol shook me up until the fortress I had built within me softened and words spilled out through my most sensitive cracks (they say that's creativity, the word spills that reveal when your guards are down).

I wrote the seedlings of this book then, a tangle of annotations, which I brought along in a folder. I don't understand all my notes, those I wrote down lazily for example; others I just don't get the meaning of, like: 'I can't hear the word *bird*' or 'I am that young girl from Shulem.' However, there is one that's completely obvious and transparent: 'Why isn't my heart made of chalk?'

I would start cleaning the balcony and scrubbing the tiles. I would organise the wardrobe and the drawers without making any noise, not wanting to wake up the neighbours. I threw away M.'s presents: seashells, a pair of gloves the same colour as my hair, a purple handbag (purple is my favourite colour), two photographs of him, wild flowers he'd brought me from the Pyrenees, and the black lace corset with the suspenders.

13

But it was impossible to get rid of everything: the urge to undertake the Bilbao-Lekeitio journey throughout the year; the added richness that M.'s subjects brought to our conversations; the feeling of redemption the touch of his lips had infused my skin with. Have you ever cried in bed, from sheer pleasure? You can't just throw that into a dump, you can't just drag it to the trash icon on your computer. There is no rubbish bin for those things, only the void of time. And meanwhile, these bits of paper.

On many other occasions, I'd go out to the garden and pull weeds, on my knees, in the dark. I'd tear up clumps of clover like a demented woman, spreading it in the process. The pit of my stomach grew quieter as my nails filled with dirt.

During the day I indulged on excess. I'd eat anything, no holds barred. One morning, back from watching the seagulls (jealous of their indifferent gliding), I stopped at the butchers and, unable to wait until I got home, entered a doorway and devoured a lump of raw bacon, tearing at it with my teeth. I bit avidly into the fat next to the callus, and bits of the reddish lean meat got stuck in between my teeth. I remember that the rain was beating against the translucent glass in the doorway, and that the sound of steps in the staircase made me scamper out of there.

At the other end of that rope was fasting. I would only eat a clear soup made of boiled garlic and parsley. But despite that, I never felt weak: when you're sleep-deprived and not hungry, the spirit of nought enters through your belly button and raises you one foot from the ground. And at times like those, even if you're neck-deep in the mud pit of your despair, you feel like a heron that flies above barren lands, travelling further and further away, to a place where the person you love, who loved you, no longer is.

DOUBLE-EDGED WEAPONS

'Don't worry, I will never ask you for anything,' I told him at the start.

It's one of those sentences that can be the starting point of a story – the last point tends to be dictated by the evolution of events. It was the white flag I waved in order not to frighten the men I wanted to be with, the strategic premise that I brandished when I still didn't care whether there was a next chapter and I made my offer straight up (I am talking about taking rolls on mattresses). But, by nature and in practice, it's tiresome to keep one's own devotion on track – let alone guide someone else's: this, of course, is impossible. What I mean to say is that there comes a point when reconciling independence with natural tendencies becomes a self-defeating struggle.

That solemn sentence is a double-edged weapon, despite its sincerity. I would voice it, hoping it would guide the future of the relationship and I would be able to try something in exchange for nothing. Entrapped by the delights of melodrama, I awarded myself the heroine's role in my own private film. *Mon style de vivre.* But I have been a very mediocre heroine, unsuited to interpret the script with sufficient dignity (dignity or coherence, to the extent to which those two terms can be said to be synonyms).

I asked M. for words. That is how I betrayed myself. That's why I left him. That's why he let me go.

'I never promised you love,' he said at the end.

THE IMPORTANCE OF DREAMS

In a way, dreams are to blame for all this.

Just like pain is a symptom of infection, nightmares are a symptom of fear. I was afraid of tethering M. to the knots of my dependence. Dreams did some important work toward helping me never give up on that idea. I didn't want to come between M. and his plans, and yet I expected him to be a bit more accommodating of my wishes. Just as I was hoping to be feather or snowdrop, somehow, I turned pebble. The irony of want but can't.

Dream Number 1 (10/06/2011) / Pregnancy
I am pregnant, happy. I am walking behind M. in the street, he is a few steps ahead (in my dreams, the men I love are always ahead of me). Someone approaches to congratulate us. M. turns around and, shrugging his shoulders, says this: 'It's not mine.'

I ascribed two meanings to the dream: one, that this thing between us was taking root in me, but that M. was staying out of it; the other, that I was taking on a disproportionate share of M.'s problems (he carried burdens he shared with me, issues from his past that kept resurfacing. We all drag heavy chains).

When I relayed it to him, he sensed that I was trying to reel something out of such a curious dream by asking him what he made of it. It was a weakness of mine, surrounding M. with words in hopes of catching an admission, something I might like to hear. I was prickled by mistrust, because sometimes his look would darken when we were together: I spied on words he never said, and that put us both on guard.

M.'s kitchen table is big. It was like an altar in full sun (I'll say that, even if I might be overstepping the threshold of twee). He told me to lie there, face down, that he had a way to dispel bad dreams. Soon after he kissed my buttocks I dug into my old wound again, with the same fishhook.

'I wouldn't want this to be our last time.'

He answered calmly: 'There is no need.'

But I persisted. If I was going to deny myself the right to be a disruption in M.'s life, I also had the right to test his sincerity, since I'm so stubborn.

'You don't need me. If we stop this thing between us…'

And he: 'Be quiet… There is no need.'

Dream Number 2 (15/06/2011) / The Window

In the second dream, M. is going somewhere, to a party perhaps. He is wearing the black shirt. He looks incredibly handsome, a hunk of a man in front of the window. I want to go with him but he doesn't want me to, he'd rather go alone. I feel an incredible pull towards him. Suddenly, I understand that the window is very dangerous for me, and I run away fast.

I woke up sweating, one of the straps in my nightie broken, out of breath and with a headache. The beams of light filtering through the holes in the blinds were like sharp fingers digging into my temples, saying 'You've lost it, love' over and over.

I was in Bilbao then. Even though we usually spoke every day, M. hadn't called me that night, or the previous one, or the one before that. I hadn't called him either (I never called him. You will understand me perfectly when I tell you that I liked being the fly caught in that web of delirium).

Water and yoghurt: I didn't feed my body anything else on those days, thinking that a cleansing diet was the way to soothe

the rancour that tortured my insides. I bought sheets. I did everything quickly: the panic of M.'s rejection, the mere thought of it, injected my extremities with the fervour of anthills.

The vein in my neck throbs still when I remember how the window spoke to me: 'Come, Meibi, come.' The message of the dream was clear: the time to jump out of the window was nigh (or, to draw a parallelism, the time to end things with M.). But I didn't have the strength required, or enough fury, to throw myself into the void. I wasn't ready to suffer his absence. Had I realised this before, I might have saved myself a few sorrows.

We still saw each other every now and then. His body was like a chalice to me, a treasure chest where to keep immutable moments, a sleek velvet rope that sometimes turned to noose, because I left the will to tighten or loosen our bond to him. I behaved against my conscience, but of my own will.

Dream Number 3 (25/07/2011) / The Suitcases

It was pointless to hope for the consolation of an admission. Back then I thought it was a matter of life or death to clear that doubt; now it's unimportant whether I go against anything that is not for my benefit.

We spent the whole afternoon lying on the sofa. I massaged his feet with almond cream (his skin is often dry, winters and summers spent in seawater will do that). He asked me: 'Why do you want those words everybody uses with anyone and for any reason, often when they barely feel them?'

It's true that the flesh sometimes has the ability to cancel everything. I sat on top of M., straddling him. I liked it like that because I could watch the tension in his face, the movement of his mouth seeking mine. He almost never looked at me in the eyes. I mention that afternoon in particular because it was raining a lot and the water flowed from me too, from my womb, in a torrent.

18

At night I had an exhausting dream. I was packing suitcases. Afterwards, I dragged them to a cabin; from the cabin to a castle; from the castle to a caravan; from there back home; and from home to the attic; and back again. I woke at dawn, completely stiff: I didn't know where to put my body, my life, my luggage. I told M. the dream in a quiet voice.

'Why are you so intent in moving things around? Leave it all alone and keep still here, next to me. Go to sleep. Can't you see I'm here?'

'I don't want you to be with me out of pity.'

'Pity for whom? I want to be with you so I don't have to feel pity for myself.'

His words didn't ring true (I couldn't imagine M. being sad without me). As always, I had begged and forced M. to hand me a crumb, and this made me bitter. I cried as we made love for the last time.

Things to develop: a) Talk more concisely about the hierarchy of the relationship; for example, about the status of inferiority (self-)assigned to the more devoted subject in the relationship when his or her expectations are not met. b) Mention other reasons that have led to the breakup with M.: his selfishness in organising free time, his overwhelming need to have me as a shoulder to cry on… c) Clarify whether it is really true that I left him or if it was a joint decision, indirectly (it was I who put the breakup into words, but if I hadn't said anything, what steps would he have taken? Maybe the very same ones, it's impossible to know). How much pride is there behind my grandiloquent 'I left M.'? Could it be that my sense of dignity made me take a false step to avoid other intimate struggles?

THE GHOST

You wake up suddenly. A bang disturbs you, footsteps on the staircase, a bird's thump against the window. For an instant you wonder whether the sound came from the dream, or if it was real, if it happened here inside the room.

Memories come at a gallop, garbled. You welcome them at first. They are gifts from the brain. The siesta in a beech wood in Mount Urbasa, the swim under the cliffs of Apikale, the swifts in Las Bardenas, M's greenish eyes. Ah, treacherous memory, how it overflies the abyss of time and space. A stab follows swiftly: 'You'll never have him that close again.'

And then, yes, memories become coarse water drops that pierce your skull. You could cut off your head and throw it across the island to feed the fish. No, there is no island here. You're in Les Landes, in a house called *Le Rayon Vert*. And a ghost came to see you. You voice his name, it tastes awful.

What message is it hoping to give you? What is it asking you to remember? You know what the visit's objective is: to impede forgetting. Because to forget is to die a little – he dies, you die. You turn in the bed. You unplug the clock. You look at the photo of your son (he's fine, with his father).

You don't turn the radio on. You don't watch TV. You don't speak to anyone. None of this does you any good.

You're afraid your reasoning is about to crack. Because you can't talk to M. about this place, about what you do and don't do, about yourself. You almost lose it when you consider that maybe he's missing you, and that's why his ghost manifested. You'd tell him: 'Lie with me, hug me.' But by sunrise there are no more signs, nothing in the breeze carries anything of yours. From the window you watch the reeds burning in the briny air.

ENUCLEATION TECHNIQUE

Enucleation is the name of the surgery required to remove an eye. It is performed in cases of severe trauma, or in eyes that have become blind and painful as a consequence of illness (when I was a high school student in Ondarroa, I used to press handkerchief against eye to alleviate a burning pain often, in the bus and in class).

It's not a complex operation. It requires seven steps, once an anaesthetic has been provided:

a) Release an antibiotic drop into each eye, and wash with physiological serum.

b) Insert the eye speculum (this is the little instrument that holds the eyelids apart, like in the film *A Clockwork Orange*).

c) Perform a limbal conjunctival peritomy for 360 degrees at 3mm from the limbus (the corneal limbus is the eye's white layer).

d) Hold each of the four quadrants with a muscle hook and cut the four rectus and two oblique (the rectus and the oblique are the tendons that facilitate eye movement).

e) Secure each rectus with a suture.

f) Insert the enucleation spoon on the side closer to the nose and push upwards forcefully.

g) Cut the optic nerve with curved scissors.

Once the cavity has been emptied, it must be bandaged and left to heal on its own for a while, because the insertion of any substitutive object is unviable until inflammation subsides.

Some of the post-operative risks include haemorrhage, muscle or tissue loss, and ptosis (the total or partial collapse of the upper eyelid).

None of that happened. Back then, when they carried out the enucleation on me, I didn't want to know anything about the surgical procedure; now, however, I can see sense in getting to know the stages of dispossession.

SELF-PORTRAIT

My reasoning capacity isn't great, but I seem wiser than I am thanks to the fluency and elegance of my speech. Often, I move towards finalising a sentence without knowing what exactly it is I am about to say, what I am actually saying. Because my intellectual ability is middling, I have neither love for, nor inclination toward, polemics, nor to dialectics. However, even though I'm not that clever, I'm practical and flexible in the domestic realm, and have been organised and effective – if not completely systematic – in the professional one. Slower than I used to be, I no longer tolerate crowds and noises like I once did.

Lack of confidence makes me waste time, I always hither and thither when trying to cancel doubts or make decisions, I much prefer it when things resolve themselves. My opinions are not fixed: I'm malleable, and sometimes side with the most articulate person in the room. There are times when my resources and experience are not enough to successfully get out of tricky situations, because I am not very good at addressing problems from a logical perspective. On such occasions, I ask for the advice of Tom or Dick or Harry, or the friend I deem most sensible and informed on the subject at the time. Interestingly, though, I read omens in nature, for example, or signals in dreams, about issues that are important to me (I might ascribe deep meaning to a daydream, for example, like a folksy Cassandra).

Most often I'm diplomatic and easy to get on with (some of my achievements came about thanks to my personal charm), I'm good at making people take my side and happy to carry out favours. Open and friendly, sometimes I'm frivolous; sometimes I take myself too seriously. I have the ability to inject my discomfort into small groups, like a poison, because I find it hard to mask my emotions. But in any case, I'll never betray; I'm no rat.

But ire, yes, I've swallowed that, gnashed bitterness with my teeth until my face turned a shade of green. I am brave and cowardly, half one and half the other, depending on the place, time and reason. Despite this, I seldom seek to humiliate or resort to mockery to attack anyone. I'm not rancorous. If I ever insult or criticise anyone, be it face to face or behind their back, it's a sign that I am slightly envious of them, or it's payback because they've played dirty with me before.

I'm a reliable person, determined and dynamic, with my ups and downs, capable of giving myself completely to endeavours that require dedication, and known to have entered the anterooms of perfectionism. I force rhythm into my work, and regenerate quickly. You'll seldom catch me staring into space (this anomalous situation is the exception).

Tender, sensitive and easily wounded by nature, I know how to be patient, generous and self-effacing. But I retrench if scolded; or rebel, if treated harshly. I tell lies under pressure or, rather, incomplete versions of the truth.

Sometimes it seems to me that life is the following: a wide-open field where laudable and righteous objectives are possible when we put effort behind them (and overcome our reluctance to share moneys). This is why even though my candidness might seem pretence to some, I am truly capable of falling into the traps of others. I can easily float along in the stratosphere, completely clueless about a problematic situation, until someone decides to burst my cloud.

I love to eat. The pleasures of the flesh are essential to me. Passionate, I am strengthened by sexual encounters, enlarged like a lascivious plant. Unfortunately, my passion is sometimes tainted by jealousy. On the other hand, even though I find unconventional models of love relationships attractive, my liberalism falls in the water at the moment of truth (I find the line between ideal open relationships and masochism a little too thin).

As far as social adaptability goes, I am totally integrated. I have accepted all rules and discipline almost without complaint. I fit easily into most circumstances. Docile, I usually want to get on with everyone, and try not to encourage enemies, at least not on purpose: I hate fights.

Every now and then I create dramas (these writings stand as proof of that). It's then that my psychological weaknesses are revealed. Self-flagellation, victimisation, a tendency to feel sorry for myself, hatred towards my failings and a misplaced sense of guilt, and feeling that I am next to nothing, provoke a bitter joy in me. I enjoy awakening the compassion and sorrow of my closest because I'm not good at suffering alone.

One of my greatest defects, the one that harms me the most, is giving too much importance to words (a bad habit derived from my profession perhaps). Sometimes I take the things said to me to the letter and end up acting bizarrely, in a twisted attempt to protect myself. On a few occasions, too, my tongue can sharpen, I don't even know how it happens, and destroy everything with a single line. A turmoil of things said to me and things I've left unsaid can fill and overheat my head easily—it's tortuous.

I'm egocentric. In general, my works ooze the stench of egomania. Even though I'll admit I should lance the boil of my narcissism once and for all, I find I face an insurmountable obstacle: I'm short-sighted, as I mentioned before. Hence my inability to widen the scope of my perspective.

And even though a sprinkly drizzle of sweet success has touched me, I'm not arrogant.

I've fought a hard, endless battle of rehabilitation within myself, improving the solid parts and repairing the broken ones. The key to my wellbeing depends on the following: keeping the different spheres of my life under control (not in the authoritarian sense, but in the sense of harmonious functioning). Awareness of this pushes me to seek balance.

Sometimes I feel claustrophobic in closed and badly-lit places, like garages for example (this might have something to do with the eighteen years I spent as the director of a textbook publishing house in a windowless office. Writing about that time feels a bit like honouring thieves who've burgled your home, but it was my fault: the trap of a job too-well-done took my son's childhood and my husband's fire in exchange for many compliments and a wonderful salary. I stole time from time. I mortgaged the sweetness of my home. I wasn't able to build a barrier between what was convenient and what needed to be done. What's more, I was so persuaded of my mission that any suggestion that I should leave the job would have seemed an offence – a consequence of badly-understood feminism. I regret not throwing a spoke into that crazy wheel sooner. By the end, I'd spend three out of every five days crying in the office, hidden behind my sunglasses. The enormity of the burden flattened me).

Like everyone else, I have contrasting aspects in my personality, which is sometimes for better and sometimes for worse. Unfortunately, I am not a person of character, you know what I mean.

Also make references to: a) Vanity, or the need to be buttered up from time to time; the security and delight that the blessings of others provoke in me; b) The relationship with my sense of self—my self-perception—and how others evaluate me.

THE MONTH OF MARIGOLDS

I miss flowers. It's a habit, keeping flowers close. When I begin to feel tired, looking at flowers revives my senses. They help me remember the mystery of small things and not forget the aesthetic side of every day. I'm at one with Szymborska: *Forgive me, distant wars, for bringing flowers home.* I miss my garden. But I'm not going to talk about it now.

I look for a florist. The shop attendant recommends marigolds. It's a September flower, the golden button. She explains that it's not only ornamental, that it's also a medicinal bloom that can heal cracks in hands and feet, and that, freshly squeezed, its juice can soothe nausea.

A perfect suggestion.

September is also the month of ferns, of San Antolin's festivities, and spring tides. For me this year, it's the month of getting rid of tidal detritus. Savour your all-or-nothing: *être*, to be—somewhere, someone; *être, pas avoir*. It must be a matter of faith, and practice. Like at the gym, I'd be grateful for an encouraging word: 'Do what you can.'

'Do you like it here?' the girl asks while she helps me bring the flowers to the car.

'At least there isn't any traffic noise.'

She stares at the piles of books spread all over the back seat.

'My name is Simone, let me know if you need anything.'

It's my third week here. The changing season is palpable in the landscape. In my eye too, it's always drier come autumn.

I observe nature more closely than before. I'm hunting for

hierophanies (I detect messages in the cadence of birdsong, in the pirouettes of dragonflies, in the green reflection of the mossy well), not to gain favour, but understanding. I know perfectly well that my behaviour follows no logic, that I am tethering on the vortex of superstition. But those signs from the landscape cause cracks to open up in my stasis: they become the starting point on the page I promised myself I'd write every day.

It stops raining and I go down to the beach. I have a quick swim, because I don't know the currents here. To my left, the lighthouse of Capbreton at the edge of the pier.

A couple emerges from the dunes. They walk in synchrony, they laugh. I feel a stabbing pain. When they removed my eye I couldn't look right or left for a while, because the movements of my healthy eye, following symmetry, would pull at the stitches inside my empty socket. My reaction when I witness the happiness of others is an echo of that.

I should have grown used to not always getting what I want; but, alas, it's impossible. Why revolt? Like the seagull who died tangled in the metallic net, I too will die of hunger, with my beak stuffed-full of the leftovers of idealism.

MAYBE

I receive a text from M. (written quickly, from work, as the abbreviations and the time at which he sent it reveal). He asks me to listen to a Janis Joplin song: 'Maybe'. Why would he ask me that? M. doesn't have a sense of the effect his actions have. Or does he.

I find the video on the Internet. Janis sings in a live concert. Immediately, the song becomes some sort of code: M. calls me Meibi. He made up that nickname for me, making a pun out of my surname and a phonetic representation of the English adverb. Since we got together, I've been a maybe, a perhaps, a we'll see. It's what I wanted at the beginning; but later, once we'd ventured deep into the adventure, the degree of probability felt a bit lukewarm.

I don't know if Janis's raspy voice is asking me for another chance, or if it's all just a homage to what M. and I had together.

I'll ask M. to listen to a song too, any other song by Janis – 'I Need a Man to Love', or 'Call on Me'. They seem to be made for me too (as much as tranquilisers or Bach flowers). But no. Enough. Forget about it. It's done.

I struggle to resist the impulse to answer.

Maybe, Meibi, Meibi, forget your demands, *baby*. Miren Agur Meabe, the half-loved column that crumbles slowly. Don't you know, you fool, that hope makes you a tool?

THE SHADOW

Although the sun illuminates everything, a shadow enters your pores bit by bit, on its way to your veins. You press your lips tight to try to block the onslaught of that terrible virus, but it settles in your mouth—a tremulous nest like an overripe fig. The tinny dark flavour spreads through your palate. You run tongue through teeth, your taste buds dry.

Your nostrils dampen. You get a hold of yourself by scrunching up your handkerchief (the handkerchief found in your pocket, the objective witness to a previous battle). Your legs are heavy. You've no option but to sit on the ground, humbled, like a dog after a beating. You know it's better not to resist it, that the shadow will spread everywhere, to your marrow, and that it'll join known and unknown realms of your being until it becomes a solid and amorphous mass.

You jump suddenly, shuddering with cold. You've been lying on the carpet for a while. It's difficult to stand up. Your body soaks up the light that comes through the window and projects a silhouette delivered from your heels. A hunched profile just birthed by that internal mass. That's why stories of people who lost their shadows invade your mind, what they say about them, how those shadows are souls that never found their place, not in heaven and not on earth.

You stare at the kitchen utensils' drawer. You'd like to stab your shadow with a knife, to split it in two, to slice it up. You don't want its company, you don't want it to follow you everywhere. But, alas, it's impossible to be free of your shadow.

31

You'd like to evoke other shadows: of a grapevine in summer, of shrimp swimming in a child's sand bucket, yours when you were younger. But they've all faded, and they're all strange, pale and elusive now. And you remain trapped by your shadow, like a drone endlessly buzzing against the walls of a glass jar.

THE PROPERTIES OF CORAL

They suggested that I could have an orbital implant instead of my prosthetic eye; in other words, to sew a scaffold onto the back muscle of my cavity and glue a thin bioceramic layer that looks like an eye on top of it. It is thought to be an excellent solution because the porosity of the material allows the eye cavity's internal tissues to grow around it.

The development of hydroxyapatite ocular implants dates back to the 90s (I've had my glass bead since 1983). The raw material is obtained from a type of Caribbean coral. Because its composition includes calcium carbonate, after a series of chemical transformations it turns into a biocompatible material, a substance similar to human bone. They've developed synthetic materials from that base, like polythene or alumina.

But putting the implant in place is extremely painful, and very expensive. I refused: should the day come when my nest can't hold my little egg anymore, I'll leave things be, that's all. That's what eye-patches are for (and won't that Saudi Arabian imam be happy; the one who promulgates that in public, women should not only cover their hair and faces, but also one eye, with an eye-patch, to avoid awakening men's ugly passions with their enticing looks).

Beyond its perfection and usefulness, the glass eye does have a downside: discharge. The more tired you are, the more gunk the eye produces. The more you touch and clean it, the more mucus you'll get. This is why I never take it off to clean, or even to sleep. Management is down to each person's organism, criteria and desires.

During the day, lubrication is essential. It's my habit to carry natural eye drops, a little mirror and Kleenex. Other than that, I visit my ocularist (the person who makes eyes) every six months to carry out a microwave-based process of hygienisation. And that's that. There is no mystery to looking after a glass eye.

WHITE WINE

I must walk. I get cramps in my legs from sitting down for so many hours. I put a raincoat on and leave the house. A squirrel leaps from branch to branch in sensing my presence. The damp ferns bordering the path look like giant hands.

In June we spent a night in the old vantage point. We climbed the hill carrying torches. It was a clear night of stars among the ungainly eucalyptus trees. M. had prepared a rough bed made out of ferns he'd cut himself with a pocketknife the day before. He'd promised me: 'I'll make us a nest of ferns.' The euphoria this type of present can induce in the short term is unmatchable. Perhaps in the long term too.

This morning the air smells of sawdust. I meet two men who are chopping up a tree in a clearing. Their dog runs towards me barking and I stand still and stare at the ground (I'm very afraid of dogs), until one of them comes over, caresses the dog and throws a chunk of wood far away.

'Do you sell wood?'

'Yes, and it's cheaper than in town. We have honey too, from our own hives— over there.'

He points at a farm on the edge of the forest. His shirt shows sweat stains in the armpits. Over the slate roof, smoke draws blue-tinged beards in the sky.

'Come, I'll walk you there.'

Their shop is in the farm's entryway, one of those beautiful old stores where you can find anything; it also doubles up as a tavern and the locals' meeting point.

'If you give me your address, I'll bring your order home myself.'

I notice the man's bony fingers as he writes down my address.

'I have opened a file on you now,' he says, winking at me.

He winks at me and I feel a prickle in my heart. Here we go again.

When I got entangled with the other one I misunderstood his signals too (the calls, the presents, the visits). They weren't clues to a premeditated game of seduction, but a reflection of his needs— and he *was* pursuing me, although he'd never admit it. I got ahead of him, inviting him first, and dragged him along into my whirlpool.

Wanting to seal any fissure through which sadness may percolate, I embraced the joyous pull of whatever happens, crossing mountains in one leap, like a giant wearing magic boots. A perfect caricature of freedom. It was a brief affair: I chose the wrong accomplice (there's no point getting into the details).

Some people show indifference to love, or to sex, and that's it. I don't know if it's a voluntary decision, resignation, laziness or some sort of achievement, something like an answer to a dare. In my case, even though I know that loving no one would save me many sorrows, if I had to forbid myself the affections of the flesh, if circumstance forced me to, that'd be it for me: I see myself turning into a pile of dry, rotting leaves, or a fish choking on the water's edge. The thought of it overwhelms me.

Tethering on the high wire of passion is my vocation; ice on one side, burning desert on the other. Even if my feet hurt, I want to take another step. And should I fall, between the barren side and the side of thirst, I'll always choose the latter.

He arrives before midday. His van's lettering reads 'Rémy et Jacques Lafitte'.

'Jacques is my brother. We own the business together.'

He piles up the wood by the fireplace and offers to light a fire. I pour us a couple of glasses of white wine as a mark of gratitude: *Jurançon de Béarn*. He explains that it's customary to serve it with a few drops of redcurrant cordial over here.

'It's too sweet for me but you might like it, it's very easy to drink,' he tells me.

'Actually, I prefer strong flavours.'

Rémy smiles at my ambiguous comment.

'What brings you here? It's not holiday season. Did you come for work?'

He looks at my hands, my fingers. My wedding band is still at home: I didn't sell it last year, when I left the publishers. I had some unexpected outlays that I couldn't meet so I put together some bits of gold (my first communion medallion, old-fashioned jewels and even some of my dead ones' teeth) and sold them in one of those Sell Your Gold places that have proliferated lately. I didn't have the heart to sell my wedding band though.

'A bit of both. To rest up and work.'

I tell him I'm a translator.

'That's why you speak good French.'

'Just about. I haven't loosened up yet.'

This time I am the one who smiles. My instinct surprises me: even at my weakest I won't let an opportunity to flirt pass me by. The secret to success: perfecting the mix of mischief and mystery.

'I have to leave, otherwise I'll be late. I've an afternoon shift, half an hour away from here,' says Rémy looking sad.

I walk him to the van.

'And this seagull—?' he gives it a kick. 'It's practically all feathers. Do you have a shovel?'

He digs a hole in the pinewood and buries it there.

'You owe me another drink.'

I nod my head. As soon as Rémy leaves, I run home to vomit.

A KISS ON THE SHOULDER

Seeing M. was wanting him.

He'd arrive around eleven and rap his knuckles on the door (we used to have dinner at mine every two weeks, on Fridays). The *Basque Geisha* would set the table up beautifully: flowers in a jug, individual placemats, dazzling salads, a seafood platter. We wouldn't touch on first seeing each other. The demands came with dinner, from him ('You haven't hugged me yet') or from me ('Where's my kiss?').

He'd approach me from behind while I was doing the dishes. He'd bury his snout in my neck, squeeze my breasts, or grab me by the hips. I liked it best when he hadn't shaved. I'd play shy, try to escape; to be honest, because I was afraid he'd find too much softness to my flesh. Despite the wavering, my body responded immediately: I was wet even before getting naked. M.'s dirty mind (especially his dirty words) roped me to a tangle of madness.

The first time would be rough (I'll never forget the creaks of my bed during our first encounter). He'd run his hand over my back, from top to bottom, the way veterinarians do to soothe animals. Afterwards, in the gallop, he'd pull my hair, softly, just enough to adjust the curvature of my waist. If I started to sweat, he'd blow on my skin. When we finished, a kiss on my left shoulder.

In the morning, when we woke up, we'd do it more tenderly, with me on top or both of us on our sides. Then I'd be anxious for a moment, trying to establish which greeting I'd hear: 'Good morning, *guapa*, I'm in no rush,' or 'Have to leave, tons to do today.' I wouldn't get up until he'd left. I'd stay in bed, holding M.'s sperm between my thighs, or sniffing the sheets in search of traces of him. Something animal bound me to him.

Burying such scenes, the way he kissed me as he said goodbye, are proving to be one of the bitterest challenges of this breakup.

I'm not going to describe M., his features or his body. But I'll describe his eyes: they're greenish-grey, and the ring around his pupils sometimes intensifies, turning gold. The most valuable assets of those eyes are these: first, that they can't lie; and second, that they know how to tend to nature. What else can I say, other than I felt stabs just by looking at him. Beauty hurts the eyes of the blind. You won't be able to understand it if it hasn't happened to you.

His virtues are crumbling now; he's so common when I judge him without compassion. Fury brings clarity, what the hell. M. the flatterer who can distinguish the song the male tit chirps to seduce the female, also looks at other women with those very same eyes. Diligent M., who will immediately lend a hand to help whoever needs help in whichever way they need it, has awarded me the zillionth place in his list of priorities, making me feel like a forgotten chamber pot in some old room. M. the optimist, who infects his friends and colleagues with joy, will never offer me unconditional loyalty. Noble M., who 'can't tell me what he doesn't feel and would like to love me the way I truly deserve,' loves freedom, that lonely, empty lot, too much. And despite all this, how many times have I soothed his fears, telling him there are no debts or regrets between us—idiot that I am.

M. is not for me. M. is not for someone like me. The heart's natural inclination can't be tamed—unless you dominate it, or force it, or blackmail it. And that's not my style.

For revision: a) Suppress details that might damage M.'s good image. b) Highlight that my interest in him wasn't purely sexual: his character, his ability to explain things that were outside my realm, his way of confronting the day-to-day and his perspective on society captivated me too.

EMPTY BUT THROBBING

I put my resistance to pain to the test. I do it by staying here and writing what I am writing.

But reality, since it's not abstract, feels as asphyxiating as a manhole cover.

I'm choking.

If I try I can escape by imagining, for example, that I am a remote place. If the sun touches me, my hair is a setting red sun in a marine landscape where my eye sockets are two atolls, empty but throbbing.

Do I realise that I am in many ways turning this stay into something mythical for myself?

Yes.

OCTOBER 7TH

It's my birthday. Forty-nine.

My son calls to congratulate me. He'll be sixteen next month. He was happy to stay with his dad for longer than usual. He's a good boy, he makes things simple, he hardly ever complains about anything. Bringing him up has been easy. Even when he was a child, I found his fortitude exemplary. So many times he'd tell me: 'Don't worry, *ama*.' A good mother would have said 'It's nothing' or 'It's OK, I'm just tired' every time he asked if anything was wrong. What I did, instead, was show him the glint of a tear— sometimes deliberately, sometimes accidentally—because I've always been a big whiny crybaby. He tells me that last week the police violently evicted the Kukutza squat, the *gaztetxe* occupied by young people. I don't listen to the rest of the news at all. He explains that he is trying to put together a band with some school friends. Knowing that he's doing fine is enough for me.

My friends prefer to contact me via email. In the summer they came to my house, each with their offering, as if they were bringing assistance to a widow with gifts of mourning. One brought me a culinary delicacy; another, nail polish; the third, pyjamas; another brought me books. A fifth one took me to see a pastoral in Larraine (hopeless, as I spent the weekend shivering and with my head buried between my knees); the sixth wrote me a prescription for antidepressants; two others called me from Donostia and Gasteiz inviting me over to have a change of scenery; another one hosted me in Ea. They all told me: 'You'll make good use of this, you'll see.' Had they been able to, they would have put me in a cradle to take turns looking after me, their little baby Mitxu. More than one offered to come to spend the day with me, but I told them I'm busy and they believed me (they always believe that).

I exaggerate emotionally, I know I do. It's impossible for me to hide my feelings even when I know that, on occasion, it goes against my own interests. But when a condition becomes chronic, it's difficult to maintain your friends' patience. By now they've run out of air to keep me afloat, and they hardly ever call. I don't have the decorum that'd enable me to move on without further ado, and I have made them feel, over and over, that they are incapable, hard as they may try, of making me look any other way. Be that as it may, I wouldn't be able to go through this without them, without the patient ears and brave souls of my Sisters of Sweet Tenderness.

I have proven to be rather incapable of confronting pain when things don't present as they should. I am a ridiculous example when it comes to self-possession. The rose of Basque poetry can't, this once, swim further. She deserves to be booed.

That's also why I ran away here, like a penitent to her cell, to digest this event that in many ways is an ideological failure (I find this collapse caused by not being loved the way I wanted to a failure). From the depths of mourning, will I emerge stronger and wiser I wonder? Should I believe in irreversibility?

Neglect is taking root around my feet, stronger and stronger roots, fed by my apathy. I can't move, although I feel a thousand cuts. And I don't want to move, because I want to write about this retreat: tangled in my very own brambles, I feel safe.

I see Rémy in the village. He invites me for a coffee. I tell him I can't, that I'm in a hurry.

Every time I look at a man, I think that no one will be able to give me the infinite pleasure M. used to give me.

I visit the street market. There is a stand where they sell animals (turtles, hamsters and so on). I don't approve of people who put birds in cages. Despite that, I buy a goldfinch. The seller warns me that it's moulting season and it won't sing yet. It's only right. I name her Janis.

M. calls me in the evening, a half-baked attempt at a call. It doesn't ring for long enough for me to pick it up.

DERMAL EFFECTS:
THE CONCH AND THE NET

Apart from being disagreeable, it's perturbing, while in public, to have your eye slip out of place or turn around and become white just because it itched and you scratched. You cover it with your hand and run fast as the wind seeking a discreet place where to readjust it. It's not a funny situation, and yet it is. There's some merit to accepting that brutal part of your physiognomy: the pinkish hollow of your eye looks like a squashed mollusc.

For a while a beggar used to board the Bilbao-Txorierri line regularly. Once he sat in front of me. I only noticed the void between his eyelids after some time, and his clam made me shiver; me, who should be more than familiar with it.

Nowadays, no one could say that I'm squeamish when it comes to examining my eyes and their surroundings. My lower left eyelid is swollen because doctors injected it with silicon to reduce the depth of the hollow and to pad up the eye-circle area. The objective of those massive aesthetic-therapeutic injections was to balance out the look of the top of my face. But due to the force of time and some wrongful calculations, the artificial folds have migrated and now my left eye-circle looks like a flat conch with reliefs that run perpendicular to my nose. That's why, when I'm very tired, if you look at the left side of my face, I look older than I am. My right eye, however, it's adorned by a network of little wrinkles—lines that pertain my age.

ABOUT THE DANGEROUS AGE

The body's clock evolves. The years demand it: sleep is reduced, muscular mass is reduced, energy is reduced. The first symptom is irregular periods (although memory's revolt comes before that). From that moment on, until the end, you irredeemably enter the dangerous age. Traditionally, it's been referred to as *the age of changes* (just like adolescence).

Lack of oestrogen causes imbalances: hot flushes, irregular heartbeat, sudden sweating, urine releases, vaginal dryness, mood swings, nervousness, abrupt sadness. Health problems can develop later on, things like osteoporosis or cardiovascular disease.

What they call 'dry eye' is one of the effects of this hormonal process. Its main symptom is itchiness, because the ocular mucosae can suffer from dryness too. In this regard, tears are very much appreciated, their effect is beneficial: when we chop onions, or when something gets into our eye, or smoke affects us—that additional flow of reflex tears is a fantastic surplus to the excess tears produced by emotional baggage. Tears help protect the eyes from infections.

It's time to consume soya. In countries in which soya is part of the everyday diet the incidence of breast cancer is lower. Nevertheless, the pharmaceutical industry sometimes uses damaging substances in their products (acetone and ethanol, among others), and their consequences on our organisms in the long term are still to be determined.

If your gynaecologist is kind, they'll make sure to provide a few recommendations: eat calcium- and vitamin D-rich foods; avoid fats; reduce the consumption of eggs, coffee and alcoholic beverages; eat more fish than meat; give up smoking; drink green tea; exercise. In general, they don't offer many explanations: they note down the date of your last period, without further specifics (a bit like when you're about to have a child and special attention and care are concentrated around the time of the delivery, and no one tells you anything about the steep hill of breastfeeding). If there is no blood flow for a year after your last period, *au revoir la jeunesse*.

I've been taking mineral capsules for a long time, one every morning. I've been constant about that at least. As from tomorrow, I'll try to have a healthy breakfast and do some exercise. Weather permitting, I'll rent a bicycle.

I've only had one period since the spring: two long traces of blood, in May, a dark, tenuous flow instead of the substantial downpours of old. It's the fifth stoppage; maybe it'll be the last. But in any case, menopause doesn't just mean that your menses stop.

When you experience a hot flush you feel like your body is made of wool. Sweat makes the hair in your temples and neck sticky. The surge lasts two or three minutes and you feel like your body exudes steam (fans end up in handbags not for romantic reasons).

Your body had already started to change. You expand, like a yoghurt pot flipped over a little plate. Your belly softens, so that if you rest on your side, it shifts towards your ribs, as if it were a wineskin. The same with the breasts. Your arm muscles dance and your legs wobble. Dark stains materialise on your forehead. Your nipples, however, get paler. The skin of your neck wrinkles (M. used to admire my neck like 'live velvet'), and when you run your hands through your face thin folds form, like they do in silk scarves. Even the sound of your skin changes: when you caress your thighs you can hear a subtle rub, and you might even release some dead skin, some scales. Hair starts to get whiter in your head and in your vulva. Your labia thin out.

47

I have stretch marks on my belly. They look like little rivers of wax. And my belly button looks like a limp, toothless mouth, similar to the mouths of mythical figures sculpted into stone bridges. My belly is the ugliest part of my anatomy. Two parallel scars of approximately ten centimetres each traverse the region above my pubis from side to side. They are thin, and not bright red, but there they are, splitting my belly in two because they had to remove my fallopian tubes as a result of two ectopic pregnancies (having my son in between the two was a stroke of luck). It is clear, then, that extirpations constitute one of the poetic *leitmotifs* of my life. It's better to see the humour in it.

On the other hand, and to list the positives, I give high marks to my skin and lips. And to my right eye, of course.

Together with what I have just explained comes the rest. Everything else, the tangle. I am not talking about an altered mental state, but about anguish—because that little question that nags us our entire lives never disappears completely ('Who or what do I need to find myself?'). Even if we can give a good answer during each phase of our lives, the longing that is the source of that question surfaces again in maturity, bothering us as soon as it's not satisfactorily answered anymore.

At the beginning of the 20th Century, Karin Michaelis called the season that hosts that intimate revolution *the dangerous age*. In her homonymous novel, a forty-something year old abandons her loving husband and comfortable life to retire to an island. She has a house built there, from which she'll communicate with the outside world through letters. In those letters, she writes about the psychiatric disorders that some women experience during the menopause transition; and in her notebook, among other things, she describes the lessons of silence and solitude. She doesn't at all show signs of depression. She chooses radical solitude not to be 'like the others.' Madness is not the way.

It sometimes happens that we seek to find a breath of joy in company and not in the refuge of solitude (even though we know that healthy eating, a job well done and physical activity are much more effective and beneficial). And since we are convinced that by now we have fewer reasons to feel afraid or to stop doing things that are important to us, we begin to invent allegories and theories that will justify our behaviour.

Climacterium. I check out Plazido Mujika's 1965 Basque dictionary's definition of *klimaterio* and find his choice of listed synonyms quite revealing: *gaitz, gaizto, galgarri, arriskuzko, galbidezko* (wrong, evil, pernicious, dangerous, corrupting). He offers the Spanish word *crítico* as further clarification of the term, too. It's funny, taking into account what I have just explained in this chapter. The notions of perdition get increasingly graphic, from disturbance to destruction, both in relation to the subject who suffers it and to the injury it can cause on others. Something is unintentionally *wrong* at first; then the loss turns *evil*; then it infiltrates, becoming *pernicious*; then it affects others, it's *dangerous*; finally, it can destroy and damage, because it's *corrupting*. Dictionaries: always so limited and always so powerful.

I look for a formal Spanish definition online. *Climaterio* is defined in the following ways in three separate dictionaries:

1. Period of life during which the activity of the reproductive organs of men and women ceases. (*Diccionario Manual de la Lengua Española Vox*, 2007, Larousse)
2. Period of life characterised by the progressive depletion of the male or female gonads. (Ibídem, 2009)
3. Phase of life during which the decay of the entire organism begins to manifest. (© K Dictionaries Ltd.)

Interestingly, a highlighted link features prominently next to the second dictionary definition. It's for a well-known brand of cosmetics and they advertise a set of products under the headline 'Menopause Innovation'. By clicking on it, you're directed to a novelty cream that combats saggy skin, presented as breathlessly and deceptively as you may imagine. The advert informs you that this is a product designed for women who, having kept utter harmonious control of their lives (through maternity, career, social prestige), have succeeded in the realms of work, knowledge and politics. Perfect Age is a product for a woman at the peak of her femininity, a woman who, at fifty years of age, has developed a sharp sense of seduction and demands a new image for menopause—a positive, non-dramatic image.

Once more, I am convinced that publicity, truly *pernicious* itself, will win over that ideal, suggestible female through the terminological shift that turns *the dangerous age* into *the perfect age*. Sweetness won't make anyone bitter, even when it's saccharine.

But note the conceptual clashes between the Basque and Spanish definitions. Sociolinguistic paradoxes depend on variables such as marketing and the moral barometer of the age.

HOW A MAMMOGRAPHY CAUSED AN ALLEGORY ABOUT STREETS

According to the X-ray, I had two shadows on my right breast, two dark almonds.

I felt that trepidation you feel when the light suddenly goes off and then returns in my gynaecologist's office. The tree I could see behind the window looked like an upright skeleton. I held back an overwhelming desire to cry by affixing my eyes to the prescription booklet and a box filled with latex sheaths.

We agreed to repeat the tests. OK. This is nothing, your tits spread between two Perspex sheets like béchamel sauce. Lean your neck back a bit, bring your trunk closer, lift your arm slightly. Very good. Hold on just a moment. Relax, don't be ashamed of your saggy breasts. That's it, very good. The metallic sound of the X-ray. Sighs of pain. Hold on.

And what if they had to remove a breast? Or something worse? How can we calculate how many caresses we have left? Our date of death doesn't show up anywhere in advance.

My husband gave me a hug when I told him. He made me feel better using clever words that consoled me and moved me. I couldn't have hoped for a better response. But it was no use. I didn't want it to be of any use.

By then, I had already started to see our story as a street, a street with several doors and a date on each door (you too must have a list of eventful dates, some wonderfully memorable and others traumatic: the day you two met; your first weekend together; the children's birth; moving home perhaps; those holidays; the fight in the middle of that damned family meal; your witless habit of mentioning, way too often, the name of a work colleague, because pronouncing their name made your heart glow; that strange evening when you treated each other with contempt in front of the teacher during a school meeting; your wife's trashy dances with friends and the night you had to breathe in the tobacco stench she brought home from the pub and impregnated the bed with as a revenge; or that time you caught a smile between your boyfriend and a waitress and you had to swallow a virulent 'Why do you have to fucking control everything?' that felt like a gob of spit on your face).

When bad days here and there turn into the poisonous air of the everyday, when bile stays in the shadows, simmering, but then boils over again and again because it's the escape route of an existential malaise, then the threat of dissemblance is there too, because while one of the two still finds their life more or less complete, the other foresees the imminence of the void. And this whole armamentarium of common but perturbing issues—which are both cause and consequence of the distancing—digs deeper into the dark, working in silence. Incomprehension deforms us in the eyes of the other: monsters multiply all the time, everywhere.

There is no way of discerning what we're doing in our rapprochement manoeuvres, whether we're the stronger or the weaker one. And because we don't know, we wander aimlessly, listening to the tapping of each other's white cane. But hesitant steps boom like bombs in silent streets (the battle of silence is a violent one) and, eventually, discouragement wins.

The circle closes up: when we're jaded, we'd like to be far away; when exhausted, it seems everything is too far away. Because there exists a distance that is a sort of compendium of the impossibility of our material being. We got entangled with another body, we caressed that face with searching fingers, ratifying the consciousness of heartbeats that we know will never synch. Maybe the other fell asleep, or became engrossed in their own thoughts, perhaps a stupid shopping list, something insubstantial, it doesn't matter. Distance overwhelms us in that indecipherable silence, and makes us feel on the verge of a precipice—unless the eyes create a bridge that brings us closer. There is no code of the skin to melt ice when those two most incompatible feelings—culpability and abandonment—are huddled up together between two lovers.

In that street for two, therefore, there are doors that are crossed in unison and doors that mark a separation. And there are stretches of wall that ooze a sticky substance, because distance is viscous, snail slime. It envelops you completely and while you fight the urge to throw up, you ask only this: to be able to continue working as always, to organise domesticity as always, to live under the same roof as always. Your request, in short: may distance not suppose, in your daily performance, a bigger burden than your shoulders can bear. It's extremely scary, in the early days, that feeling of distance making you feel so vulnerable.

If distance has released the eggs of unloving within your chest already, all you can do is choose one of these two options: either you ignore its cold sludge, making a supreme effort to make happiness find a corner in your street (that's the built-in tax of conventional lifestyles: to keep on moving forward repeating mantras such as 'This happens to everyone, living together is hard' in your head); or you leave aside what is expected of you and open the door you see in that allegorical street of life, that dangerous door that beckons you, and you cross it at your own peril.

If you've felt time running away from you, anxiously, like steam from a freezer, you may decide to get rid of one costume to put another one on while you tell yourself: 'I am a woman,' as if it was the first time that line has been voiced in its full meaning.

If forgiving and asking forgiveness is now akin to dragging an iron ball tied to your ankle, start doing things for yourself, seek something (it might be another man's hand) that will lift you up from the ditch of sadness, of disdain, of boredom, of ceding and conceding, of fear, of resentment and discontent.

I think we were lucky. When our white canes started to clink together in the mist, we agreed to hit pause to save the ashes of our beautiful past: 'You deserve it, I deserve it.' Good wishes replaced love and took over its place.

Voilá the tale I tell myself. The tale's justification, my need to squeeze everything out of life. If everyone who experiences the threat of illness or goes through a crisis did what we did, what would become of this planet—it'd be chaos.

THEORY OF THE LITTLE
BOX OF CHEESE WEDGES

In the end, the diagnostic after the second mammography was good. The shadows weren't tumours, but calcifications that needed to be closely monitored (and that was the end of the story—so much hassle and alarm about nothing). Meanwhile, my own statistics led me to outline the theory of the little box of cheese wedges. It goes like this:

'Life is a little box of cheese wedges in which not every portion has the same sell-by date. In mine, there are four that need to be replaced: my love life, my profession, where I live, and poetry (believe it or not, back then I was going through a barren patch, creatively speaking, although all these events I mention here soon became fertile literary seedlings); the other three portions are still fresh: my son, my friendships and my utopia.'

'…?'

'To become increasingly more Queen and Commander.'

'But don't little cheese boxes contain eight portions?' my friends asked.

'Let's suppose that the eighth is a wild card, a portion reserved for the novelties, the ability to welcome change … the power of being water. *Be water*, my friends.'

Now I'm ashamed by my shallow attitude. How many times must I've looked like an idiot. And more so after what happened with M., when I realised that break ups of the mind and break-ups of the heart don't necessarily take place immediately, or even simultaneously.

I feel pity (and a little admiration) for people who never ever lift the lid of their little box of cheese wedges, those who never even attempt to take off their mask because, after such a long time and so much effort, they've merged so well with their costumes— all those wife, daughter, mother outfits. A warm round of applause for those who are able to delimit the alpha and omega of their happiness so succinctly. Despite everything, and no matter how much they may dye or restyle their hair, does that unmentionable ideal ever stop pecking at their heads? Maybe they find a legitimate means of sublimation in department stores. Because you need a degree of bravery to allow walled-in feelings to burst through, and also the lucidity to rearrange the terms of that most important of questions (in other words, to transform 'Who or what do I need to find myself?' into 'How do I want to live now?'). That's what Adrienne Rich asked the very same Adrienne Rich: 'What you intend to do with the rest of your life?' Suspecting that the answer is on the other side of that unknown door, some will say 'stop' and others 'go,' and the consequences of one or the other will be absolutely incomparable.

I know women who take on a lover at this age. They've told me that having a lover seemed to them a way of attaching value and respect to themselves. Most times that affair is the first and only one, and it has a somewhat architectonic objective, something like a complementary pillar to sustain the frame of the everyday. Love can be the reason too. One way or another, it seems to be a survival strategy: relationship B is a point of support for life A; and the need to hide situation B, a stimulus to protect circumstance A.

Many hide that chapter, like someone who'd bury their treasure in the forest. A few bring it out into the light if there is no other option, or when they feel ready to abandon their husband (if the husband hasn't left them first, as soon as they found out; although there are also devoted husbands, willing to start all over again: anything for their wife, or for the children). A few will leave without taking a penny, without demanding or explaining anything. Rare exceptions aside.

As for men, I have the feeling that for most of them it's just easier not to worry about the state of their little cheese wedges, thanks to the following options: football, beer, *mus* games, weed, sport, dinners in their gastronomic societies, success or political power, and whores. Rare exceptions aside.

Carolyn G. Heilbrun puts it like this in her essay: 'Most women, I think, transform our need to be loved into a need to love, expecting therefore, of man and of children, more than they, caught in their own lives, can give us.' Next to a man happily reading a newspaper there is, usually, a frustrated woman. Obviously, the noun *newspaper* can be substituted by many others. The meaning of this is that if the passion-adoration of a man towards something is not strong enough to include a woman in it, that woman, sooner or later, will end up embittered—and who knows what might happen after that. That's Alice Munro's perspective in one of her short stories in *Open Secrets*. The title says it all.

REASONS FOR LOSING AN EYE

There tend to be two main reasons for losing an eye: accident or disease.

A pupil of mine had a tumour in his retina in the years I was a teacher (I take this opportunity to offer an example of childish spontaneity: 'What happened to your eye?' the kids would ask. They didn't expect my answer).

A fisherman from my brother's circle of friends took his own eye out as he was trying to release a knot in a net with a knife that flew upwards with all of his impetus behind it.

An administrator in the Solokoetxe health centre told me that her brother in law suffered terrible wounds in a car crash and won't remove his sunglasses at all. He's not coping well.

There are those who have lost an eye in a terrorist attack. Or in a demonstration.

While we're on the subject of revolution, there's a great example in silent cinema, the massacre in *Battleship Potemkin* (Einsenstein, 1925). The Tzar's Cossacks shoot at people in retaliation against the Bolsheviks. A bullet hits a woman who is running, pushing a pram, right in the eye. The pram slides down the great steps of Odessa, and so on. The mother's destroyed face is worth seeing.

Claudia Massin deals with the need of completeness when she writes that the result of everything we lose is a cipher, an individual one; and that when we lose something that is ours, something that we ought not to have lost, our cipher turns forever inexact.

The waiting room of my ocularist is always filled with inexact ciphers. And when it comes to draw the balance of losses vs. gains, it can't be said that one eye's deficit means a surplus for the other; not in terms of vision, and not in terms of shine.

THE LETTER

Vieux Boucau, October 14th 2011

M. now and always:

Time died, and it's resurrected. You'll understand me in a moment.

The clock in the hallway turned up on the floor today. The hook came loose, and one of the hands broke when the clock fell. From now on, that incomplete clock won't be able to tell time: it'll be inexact forever. This unexpected event has woken me from my anaesthetised state, making me blink. My awakening involves writing this letter.

These last few days the weather has been horrendous. You've probably been in the breakwater admiring the waves. You may have even gone for a swim. You used to say that you have to be able to measure how much you can withstand the swell. That the undertow pushes you out at first and you feel encouraged, thinking you'll swim out, but that when the wave comes down again, it traps you like a puppet made of corn leaves. With the third wave, you sink.

The storm dragged branches to the beach. I brought some home to sand down and put them in a big empty flagon I found in the junk room, covered in dust. I've turned remains into ornamentation. That's what I do, make good use of whatever the beach or fate put in my hands.

Our story started at the beach, our first exchange of words in October, two years ago now. Isuntza was covered in seashells. When you approached I assessed your height, your teeth and your nails. You didn't seem dangerous to me, sexually I mean (interesting, aren't they, the whims of love). You spoke openly and I was touched by your concerns (those problems, that old burden). Therein lies the downfall of the compassionate woman.

60

Later you told me that you had noticed me before, swimming, reading or scribbling on some papers. That you had wondered what it might be like to make love to a woman like me. What did you mean by 'a woman like me'? You meant a woman in the dangerous age. A woman who knows how to be alone. A woman that has stories to tell. That's what you meant.

There's a portolan chart in the living room of this house, an old navigational map with colours, signals and signs organised according to some hierarchy. It reminds me of you. Whenever we laid down next to each other, I paused on each of the moles on your back, dozens of tiny brown islands, telling you: 'This is my territory.' I'd cover your back with kisses thinking that I'd be able to conquer your heart with my lips (you entered mine with all those unrepeatable vocatives and the kisses you planted on my belly). The distance between your muscles, the angle between your neck and shoulders, the length of your column and the surface of your glutes were terra cognita for me; your internal territories, not so much. And now I feel like a shipwreck on her raft between these sheets, aimless, compass-less, as if the order of values of my route had been thrown into disarray because I lost the map that was you.

Do you know what the local touristic slogan is? Une autre saison. If it's true, as cartography says, that we're perpetually discovering new places in the universe, come back to mine, and come back here to Les Landes: you'll find a woman on the beach. I am your femme à l'autre saison.

Meibi

I hesitate in front of the postbox and, in the end, don't send the letter. I am revolted by my prudish lyricism, by my sanctimonious attitude, my sickly-sweet adoration, the bad habit of attributing symbolic meanings to straightforward reality, my ever-so-basic play on words.

How could I have forgotten that the bodies of imprudent swimmers don't always turn up?

My weakness, a slacker, tries to fool my will.

But, what is my real aim? What is the point of the whole litany of my letter? What price must I pay: shame or regret?

I burn the letter. Not without making a copy first: I'm under the spell of my own ink.

ANIMATION GASCONNE

There's an *Adrenaline parc* in Moliets. The leaflet advertises risk-free fun: *quad, body-board, paint-ball* and *skate*. An unbeatable proposition for business celebrations, anniversaries or farewells, open every day from 2pm to 7pm from April to September. Participants must be at least fourteen years old. If it were open M. would have a blast. He's quite the child really.

And he'd quite happily admit that assessment (being childish), which is insulting for most adults. 'We should all know how to be kids even when we've grown up,' he'd said. 'Why not?'

I see the seaweed collectors almost every day. A group comes from Hossegor on foot, a tractor along with them. There must be a research centre that organises the visits, I don't know where. Some local artisans use the seaweed to make soaps, mixing them with oils and natural fragrances. I should buy some to gift to my friends when I return.

During a quick visit to the multimedia library I see a mural representing the flora and fauna of the Atlantic coast. It shows how the contours of the Aturri river have gradually evolved to become this landscape of forests and dunes. The predominant livelihoods are a consequence of it: the wood industry, the commercialisation of geese and geese-related products, and tourism (including everything related to surfing).

A paradise for M., the veteran eternally young surfer. Riding waves for him is a way of being in the world. He started not long ago, well into his forties. A healthier way to deal with the adversities life will throw your way. Every time the roaring sea towers over him he tells himself: 'If these walls of water don't swallow me, neither will the ditches in firm ground.' That's why I call M. *marraxo*, because he *is* a shark that never stops swimming, because he'd die if he stopped; and because although his skin has weathered the blows of many harpoons, he remains an upright man who withstands.

I cycle all the way to Leon lake, about 10 kilometres away. I push the pedals hard, because of the wind. I walk barefoot on the shore. I like feeling the sand and the pine needles under my feet. If M. were here, we'd rent a kayak to cross the lagoon.

There is a small hotel here, a really cosy one. I always liked it, from the first moment I saw it. I remember an old poem of mine in which I wrote that I'd like to write my initials on the sand, or my phone number on the window of a car. When I wrote that, aeons ago, I was thinking precisely of this hotel: of the possibility of meeting up with a mysterious date and contemplating dusk and dawn from a bedroom, the violet edges of the water first, then the red ones. I always award myself the role of the girl in the perfume advert in my fantasies.

A GLASS EYE IS A METAPHOR TOO

Why do I talk about all this? It's a challenge I set myself, because of an editor who baited me a long time ago. I thought it was funny.

'Are you kidding me? You can't be serious.'

'Think about it … your glass eye might inspire something.'

'If that was the thing that makes me a writer, all right, but … oh, do you mean metaphorically?'

'Not at all; doesn't it affect you in your everyday life, the fact that you only have one eye? Write about that, but do it with the precision of a razor blade.'

'Are you trying to imply that I'm cloying?'

Afterwards he mentioned a short story by Castelao, '*Un ollo de vidro*'. The narrator tells the story of how he lost an eye following a cockerel's brutal peck.

And, going back in time, a satirical poem by Jonathan Swift in which Corinna, a graceful damsel who, on her way to the market, drops her eye and has to get down on the ground to pick it up (at least that's what I understand with my very basic English).

Another time he sent me a message recommending that I read Curzio Malaparte's *Kaputt.* Among the things that he experienced during WWI, he explained how once, in an inn, they showed him a basket filled with eyes torn off war prisoners.

I recalled Koldo Izagirre's book, *Sua nahi, Mr. Churchill?* The passage about Aitzol, to be precise, how Hidalgo explodes his eye when he hits him with a wrench the night before he's shot by firing squad.

I discovered Henri later, the farmer boy who, seduced by Bonaparte's charisma, wanted to be a drummer in his army but had to be content with being his cook; the young man left one eye as well as his heart on the frozen steppes of Austerlitz. That character was created by Jeanette Winterson (by the way, in her novel *The Passion* we can find sentences as wise as this one: 'You see, I like passion, I like being among the desperate').

What do I care about all those realistic examples of literary eyes. In my case, the eye has a double dimension: one is real, because it's a mark of my identity (don't tell me you hadn't noticed anything, my left eye looks much smaller...); the other, metaphorical, because I have chosen it to represent all the losses of my life.

I don't know where this experiment that I began on September 9th 2011 will lead me. I don't know how long it will go on for, or how many arguments it'll hold. It's mid-October now.

Something to take into account. I spoke to the editor in question just a while ago. I've given him an overview of the plot: 'The driving force of the narrative is a broken passion and, the glass eye, a symbol. You know it's a characteristic of mine, one that in this instance will represent the bits of me that are damaged. I'll deal with the subjects of age and so on, too.'

His reaction disappoints me: 'So, are you writing about an old woman?' I wanted to tell him to fuck off, so exhausted I felt by the narrowness of his squalid point of view. And he wasn't being ironic, or attempting to provoke me as he always does. He spontaneously pre-judged and devalued the process and conflicts of my character.

Maybe this text will end up in a drawer. Or in the rubbish bin, since rubbish is, by definition, everything that is rejected, everything that results from an activity of zero value.

I'm going to get on with what I started, however.

THE TEMPTATION OF PLUS

A friend calls me. She doesn't know where I am; she doesn't ask, and I prefer that she doesn't. She needs someone to listen to her drama and I'm known for being an attentive listener.

She tells me that she fell in the morning, that she doesn't know how, that she suddenly found herself on her knees, washing blood off the floor with a rag.

'You know, making sure everything is perfect before I leave the house,' she says with irony, making me smile. 'Well, that was later, when I came to and thought: *What the fuck am I doing?* And I went to the bedroom like a zombie and shouted at my husband: *Give me a towel, I'm bleeding! Hurry up!* He woke up with a start, as if I'd thrown a bucket of cold water at him.'

In hearing about the rag I remembered the woman who suddenly appeared on the neighbourhood pavement. She was wearing a pink dressing gown and the bottle of Windex had formed a blue puddle next to her exploded head.

'She's not the only one,' reported a customer in the corner café. 'They jump with a rag in their hands to make it look like they were cleaning the windows ... to make sure that the family can cash in the life insurance, of course.'

I stared at the ground to disguise the shock I felt at the rationality of the explanation. The concentric circles the coffee had left in the bottom of the coffee cup looked like a closed road, a labyrinth filled with mythical names. For example, Sylvia, who put her head in the oven after making breakfast for her children; Alfonsina, who gave herself to the sea after sending her goodbye to a newspaper;

Virginia, who walked into the river with her coat pockets filled with stones; Anne, who choked in the garage with her car's carbon dioxide fumes; Alejandra's Seconal pills; Marina and the rope around her neck; Ingeborg and her candles; Karin Boyer asleep on a rock, the sweetness of a syringe; Ana Cristina Cesar, was it a shotgun or did she jump from her parent's terrace?; Tove Ditlevsen, more sleeping tablets; Reetika Vazirani, haemorrhaging out of her open veins; Florbela Espanca, Amelia Rosselli, Danielle Collobert, Nilgün Marmara. The deaths of those women sparkle like precious stones: suicide removes superficial annexes from their biographies. As a result, every detail gains significance.

'I told him to bring me a bath towel, that I was dizzy ... the girls were asleep, thankfully. It was only ten past seven still.'

My friend is still talking. I can perfectly imagine the situation: baking soda in the bathroom cabinet, hairpins, eczema cream. The blood has left a brownish stain on her nightgown, like it did moments before on the kitchen rag (like I did today on the sanitary towel; I hadn't had a period in five months).

While she talks to me I start to think crazy things: whether suicide could help to raise the profile of my life and works, add a certain plus to one or the other. Crazy things indeed. The arrogance of someone who's never had to experience what it really means to feel truly naked and empty in her own flesh, someone who doesn't know misery, exile, hunger, being forced to leave children in orphanages, concentration camps, psychiatric hospitals, cancer, state violence... They had nothing left to live for. 'There are only two options,' says Joumana Haddad, 'either you run away from your own death, or you tame it.' Or not.

What are the rightful criteria to hold on to life?

What kind of death would I choose? To wait for a train inside a tunnel, curled up between the rails like foetus. I turn into a babe-in-arms each time this pain hovers over my shoulder like a scary, clawed animal.

Igor Estankona, in a poem in his book *Anemometroa*, provides a brilliant metaphor to describe desperate love. He says that to love so-and-so is to jump from a sugar tower. A sugar tower, the image of sweet but crumbling love, a love whose peak is reached by climbing over scaffolds assembled with great effort, using harnesses that won't hold cowardice.

The woman in the pink dressing gown (perhaps a very much loved and pitied mother) let herself fall from a ninth floor flat on Zabalbide Kalea, my street. She must have kept a dungeon inside herself, or an endless spiral staircase, definitely not pinnacles of honey. Where does a person who doesn't have the will to live find the courage to approach the edge of a window? Maybe she was an unstable person. Or maybe she had an incurable disease. Or maybe she was chained up somewhere in the depths of the labyrinths of the dangerous age. Her life lost all sense. Or maybe what she lost was the sense of having sufficient strength to confront it.

My friend doesn't see how distracted I am, making up a parallel story that is more attractive than the story of her syncope.

'Twelve stitches, my dear. I must have crashed against an open drawer. In hospital they said it was most likely a drop in blood pressure but, believe me, a whole documentary on tumours ran past my head. Can you believe I started listing the things I need to do on a piece of paper; I looked for my lawyer's number, I wrote a draft of a letter for my daughters...

Why this female predisposition towards organisation, and the instinct to protect our own no matter what?

I look at my feet. I feel like I am sliding down a horizontal slope. At the same time I start to think what is it that I would want to clean up: all the glass, the lamps, or the attic. My computer's hard drive—that definitely needs a good sweep.

I lie: I never ever delete anything I write. I keep it all, hoping that those meandering lines will sooner or later find a text in which they can settle. This metamorphic writing soothes me until I reach the point of accepting the challenge of the empty page.

'Go to bed with a magazine, rest up, demand to be pampered...' is my advice to my friend.

I know that I've just spoken nonsense. I know I'm thinking many stupid things. I know that it's absurd to pretend to build up a story with my sorrows as starting point.

We say goodbye. I look around me. Then I look at my feet again. They're frozen. I hit the floor with my heels to make sure, once again, that I am where I should be.

IN THE MOUSE TRAP

It's dark by four thirty. Autumn in Les Landes has nothing to do with what I knew. I was waiting for it. Days and nights are endless. Beyond the peace that silence brings, what I am discovering here is resentment towards solitude, towards the way quietness eats away at you. I am prisoner of the mousetrap I made for myself.

Are you finding such torment hard to believe? Well, we commit extravagant nonsense such as this one and worse when we are hooked on someone (learning to deal with these conflicts more sanely would be a whole other story). You don't want me to confess that what I feel for M. is the strongest thing inside of me. You want to read that I have another passion, a greater, more profound one: writing for example. You believe that such a thing would strengthen my will to move forward.

M. calls twice. He says he's worried. I feel the burble of blood in my ears. That he doesn't need me as much as I need him. 'You're not angry, are you,' he says. The gash between us is still there, burning red.

'At least send me a message every now and then,' he asked the last time. I let out a bitter guffaw. He's not going to get missives like mine from anyone, that's for sure. 'I look at your old messages while I eat my sandwich at the factory, or when I go to bed. There are more than two hundred, Meibi, two hundred flowers.' All right then, all things considered it looks like I wasn't a mirage then, like the little girl from Shulem who, admiring a king from the distance, threw her verses in the air—in vain, her words like petals.

NA NGA DEF, XARIT?

Yesterday someone knocked on the door. I didn't attend, I thought I'd imagined it. They insisted, so I looked out of the window. There was a Senegalese man outside, with a big bag on his shoulder.

We had a cup of coffee in the kitchen. He explained that he sold more if he went door to door and that he travels from town to town by bus. I asked him how to say some things in Wolof.

'*Ça va, mon amie?*'

'*Na nga def, xarit?*'

He made me a résumé of the story of his life. He had a warm smile. It did me good.

I bought some socks from him, for my son. And a bracelet, an Indian-looking trinket with brown and pink enamel combining geometric and flower designs. Although I rarely have the impulse to buy myself presents, I picked it up without giving it a second thought: it had a portrait of my Janis—a chubby bird on a branch. It even had the pinecones of the *forêt des Landes*. The bird is happy on its branch, beak closed. Its eye is a minuscule black dot. I had a feeling that it was watching me, waiting to show me something, like creatures do in fairytales.

A BRIEF HISTORY OF OCULARISTICS

Notwithstanding its precursors, it can be said that ocularistics, as a specialty, started in the 18th century—first in France and, a bit later, in Germany.

Auguste Boissonneau is considered the father of ocularistics. He carried out tests with multiple materials, and glass proved to be the most readily tolerated by his patients. His work had an enormous influence in the development of the science of artificial eye-making; so much so, that at the start of the 19th century, German surgeons pushed for further research on the subject with the objective of stopping French monopoly and coming up with a national product.

There was once, in the beautiful Turinga-Lauscha region, a young artisan who produced glass. His name was Ludwig Muller-Üri and he built eyes for dolls. One day, having copied French techniques and combined them with his own, he developed a great advancement in the prosthetic eye industry. He was awarded lots of prizes in international scientific exhibitions and, thanks to him, the first German workshop for human artificial eyes was born: *Erstes Deutsches Atelier für Künstliche Menschen Augen*.

But I am fonder of the French Auguste than the German Ludwig, because he made lots of trips around Europe to tend to his different customers, both military and civilian. His son used to accompany him, to lend a hand. He shared his knowledge through infinite articles and books. One example among many is *De la restauration de la physionomie chez les personnes privées d'un oeil ou Exposé d'un nouvel oeil artificial à double échancrure interne*

(Paris, 1858). Besides, he was a naturalist, an ornithologist. He identified lots of species of birds.

However, in the 20th century, after WW2, the United States took over the field. Acrylic ocularistics was born, which quickly gained ground over the traditional *oeils de verre*.

THE MIRROR

I am looking at the front cover of an edition of *The Book of the City of Ladies*, written by Christine de Pizan in 1405. The author describes a city that is invincible because the stones with which it was built are the women of the past, and the materials used to finish it, mortar and ink. The illustration, by Anastasia (the artist that the French Court put at the service of Christine) captures my attention.

A Renaissance lady sits in front of an easel. In her left hand, a round mirror reflects her face; with her right, she holds a brush and paints her self-portrait on a canvas.

The image of the woman appears three times, therefore: as a subject, on her chair, and as an object in the mirror and in the painting. In this triple game of reflections, this notion is confirmed: self-observation can be both the origin and the objective of creation. At the same time, it suggests the speculative nature of art to me, the way observer and observed are mutually and endlessly reflected.

Within grasp of the painter, a few bowls containing pigments, a wooden box, a bodkin and another object that I fail to identify at first but see clearly now: another hand mirror, with a handle, face down on the table. On the back of that mirror there's diffuse gleam, dark blue, white and red, which corresponds with the background of the painting, the skin of the woman and the colour of her tunic. In other words: in some way, the mirror that carelessly rests on the table also reflects what the author is working on with such care and caution.

The lady puts the finishing touches on her portrait resting the tip of her brush not on the hair of the figure on the canvas, or on her forehead, not even on her chest, but on her mouth, co-conspirator of words. By analogy, my eye assigns obvious interpretations to the elements in the scene: the canvas is the space of writing; the bowls of pigment, the biographical aspects that influence it; the bodkin, the will to excise any excess of form or content; the wooden box is the receptacle where the jewels of the past, of memory, are kept.

The attitude of the painter who scrutinises herself in the mirror shows me that I must observe the person that I am with detail. Her eyes and slightly downcast head transmit the tranquillity of those who long for nothing. Her (our) only desire is to see and reflect us completely.

And what does the reversed mirror represent? The ability to reflect only part of reality. Or, maybe, everything we can't see through the mirror of consciousness. Or what we can't see because of our biography or our genetic carapaces. Or the things we don't want to see. Maybe that mirror represents the others, those who complete the picture of who we are.

How perplexing, the meaning of that oblique mirror.

I know what I'm doing. I'm clawing into my pain to get some yield out of it.

I will never hold back from admitting that licking my wounds has brought me some benefits. And you can criticise me again now, accuse me of taking on the role of damsel in distress, and say that all this gibberish looks like a therapeutic exercise, the written version of a reality show.

Likewise, I won't bury my head in the sand if you reproach me for echoing an outdated pattern: to find beauty in pain was the sin of the women who preceded us, as pathetic a flaw as that of making ire acceptable. My attempts at avoiding sentimentality are pretty unsuccessful half of the time. And dealing with the evident has no merit (I blush at the mediocrity of my reflections, I can admit that myself).

Only I know the extent to which I'm honest and how deliberately I omit some details: what's not applicable must not be given away; and, *au contraire*, the trivial must be maximised if it feeds the point, or the need to know. You must agree with me on that one.

That's why I'm telling you that this text is not a pier, or a bridge, or a lighthouse, or a home, or a road with foundations made of iron and cement, but a glass mirror with a patchwork frame.

The *patchwork* technique consists of sewing loose pieces together; it's not to be confused with the *matryoshka* concept. Just like the Russian dolls are hidden one inside the other, the author too will hide within the strata of their work. Not I. Many writers keep their image within wraps, aware of the immunity not dangling bait before the predatory eyes of the reader can guarantee. Not I.

PROSTHESES IN CASES OF CONGENITAL PATHOLOGIES

So there are quite a few of us in the ocularist's waiting room.

Once, I heard a child cry. They were shrieks of terror, the fear provoked by a battle already lost shaped into tears. Mother and child came out of the consulting room shortly after, the child with his head keeled over his mother's shoulder, exhausted. He can't have been but three years old. It was my turn next.

'Poor thing, he's had a terrible time,' I said to the doctor.

'He was born without eyes.'

Cases of microphthalmia are one in a thousand. It's a congenital malformation of the foetus that means that eyes, eyelids or even tear ducts never develop. The newborn's eyes will never be any use: they'll forever be two opaque buttonholes. But installing prosthesis is not feasible until the growth and development of cranial bones has concluded completely. Specialists believe that such a radical repair is essential for the successful socialisation of people with this condition.

SHE WHO NEVER ABANDONED ME

Every now and then I have a good dream, a kindness from my instinct of preservation. Paltry protection, but valuable for times of vigil. I dreamt of my mother tonight. Soon it'll be ten years since she died. In the dream, *ama* was taking the buttons off a dress (she owned a clothes shop her whole life).

'A way of fixing clothes that are too tight,' she told me. 'The fewer the buttons, the better you'll breathe.'

I saw *ama* as she was in her fifties, not the faded woman she was when she died.

'Of course you'll get through this,' she added, 'you're my daughter.'

Tonight I slept eight hours for the first time since July.

Joyce Carol Oates, in her novel *Mother, Missing* writes that the destiny of mothers is to remember. That they remember things only they know and, also, things that absolutely no one else cares about. Such things, when mothers leave, go with them: the buoy that marked your place by the sea goes. Who else can remember the scribble I drew on the wall when I started to go to school, the exact corner where I drew it; who will remember the time I took a coin from her purse without her permission. Mothers are the memory of childhood.

'When life is bitter you have to swallow it by the spoonful, like medicine.'

Ama interpreted sorrows her way, and was consoled by the thought that upsets, in the long term, brought along some sort of goodness. Like so many of her generation, she wasn't used to doing what she wanted, but what she had to.

I made her tell me what I needed to hear:

'You'll feel short of air, but you won't choke.'

Fear of my possible blindness ate away at her happiness since I lost the eye. Yet, out of the ruins of that crumbling fortress she amassed this naïve joy, like children make balls out of loose bits of old play dough. She had reason to worry: my paternal grandmother was blind. She lost one eye in an accident, when whitewash fell out of the kitchen ceiling and burnt her eye; the other she lost as an old woman, due to hypertension. I must have inherited my glaucoma from her, like I did my loquacity. Her middle son was that uncle of mine whose eye was blown out by a petard (this concatenation of coincidences might sound like parody, but I think it's pertinent to mention all this).

My *ama* made pilgrimages with her little ugly-eye daughter to every ophthalmology temple until the day of the irrevocable decision: we needed to extirpate. Despite all those visits, there's no doubt I would have lost my eyesight a long time ago if she hadn't forced me to go for one last consultation— since by then I refused to accompany her, bored of always hearing the same diagnosis. Everywhere they said there was no cure for my sick eye but, until that last visit, nobody had warned us about the very real and immediate risk of losing the healthy eye. *Ama*, who had always felt an affinity for Saint Lucy because she is the patron saint of seamstresses, developed a fervent devotion for her from that point onward.

My worst memory after the enucleation is not, funnily enough, the gigantic cotton ball plugging my cavity, but the catheter; the horrific and repeatedly failed attempts by two clueless nurses to introduce a rigid tube into my urinary tract. With the years, *ama* and I would laugh remembering the things we lived through in that clinic in Zaragoza.

Even though she wasn't that strong, my *ama* stood up to everything. Tonight she told me: 'Have faith.'

If you bring a finger close to a baby they hold on to it, because that piece of flesh for them is something like a rope the world is extending to them. Dreaming with *ama* made me understand that there are no previous patterns to base the assemblage of our lives on. The things that happen to us are a collage, fragments of a larger story that gains meaning as the story completes: life is a dress that looks increasingly better as its parts are sewn together. I feel grateful for my ability to take this dream as a crutch to help me walk in the real world.

Questions: do the references to my mother sufficiently manifest that she was an exemplary woman who taught me that perseverance is the weapon with which we break through the frontier between weakness and strength?

'The Mother' is a recurring theme in my works. If this text were to be published it could invite a too-easy déjà-vu, imply some sort of obsession, reflect an irreplaceable void. I don't think it's any of those things. However, not cutting the psychological umbilical cord could be, ultimately, a strategy to console myself.

SCARS AND THE REST

Time needs to rot memory in order to be able to speak of the past. Everyday events gain sparkle (they become worthy of mention) when recollections ferment.

We had a clothes shop in Dendari street. It was a dark, long space, filled with wooden shelves. Right across, there was a fountain with a date written on top: 1888; us kids would drink there in the pauses between our playful comings and goings.

As a child, I was fascinated by dental braces and vaccination scars. I wanted scars on my skin. I thought they signalled that the people who had them had lived through memorable experiences, that they were the testimony of wild adventures I hadn't had. I would contemplate the ugly mess a wound had left in my friend's knee with admiration.

'A soda bottle exploded on me,' she'd explain proudly.

The circular vaccination scars I saw in the naked arms of my mother and other women during the summer made me think of tiny moons or yummy pancakes made of flesh. Playing nurse, I would draw marks on the forehead and arms of my favourite doll, with a pen. In my eyes, she seemed older with those drawn-on signs. Not giving it a second thought, I imprinted on her rubber skin the wounds that the world hadn't inflicted on me yet, and which, with time, have become an excuse for my literary endeavours.

Once, I received a present of a first aid kit – a zippered, fake leather case with a red cross at the top. The toy made us toy with its multiple possibilities: the little silver scissors, the black phonendoscope, the bandages, the little box of (sugar) pills and the rubber needles proved to be extremely stimulating objects with which to begin to explore our bodies. That first aid kit became our first conduit for sexual experience (which might have something to do with the fact that, to this day, medical exams are one of my erotic fantasies). We used to play in the back room, little girls in blue school uniforms and white socks. As soon as my friends and I arrived from school, I'd kiss my mum, grab my snack from a drawer in the counter and go through the shop, all the way to the back. The mere fact of closing the door behind us made us feel that we were in our own private lounge. Since my mother couldn't really pay us much attention while she had customers and, besides, she was always mending or sewing something, we were free to do as we pleased in there.

On the floor of the back room there were several fabric rolls, of the kind sold by the metre; fabrics rolled around rectangular, hard cardboard tubes. Most of them were discreet, sailors' blue nankeen or sombre prints for mourning clothes—but one was special, a red and white cloth in a flower pattern, of the kind used to make mattress covers, each side a negative of the other. That's the one we used as a stretcher in our medical examination games. I remember a friend's hands sliding up and down my torso, pausing on my still-flat nipples. I happily obeyed her orders: 'Stick your tongue out,' 'Open your legs,' or 'Touch my navel.' I also remember the blunt tip of the plastic scissors in my anus, and the pressure of gauze on my groins as if healing some wound, patting dry a wetness that back then was impossible.

Although obedient, I was, at times, a know-all; I wasn't arrogant, but I was vain; I wasn't spoilt, but I was a bit lippy; I was delicate, but not whiny. I think the disaster of my eye was a big lesson in humility. Ever since turning thirteen, the pretty little girl had to admit that she carried something that could repel people. I had a mantra I would repeat in difficult times ('Although I'm normal, I'm special too'). Voicing it was an ejaculatory prayer for my psyche—just like scars are, to flesh, a confirmation of pain.

Deploying tricks to manage the things that fuck us up is a non-transferable process.

When *amabitxi,* my godmother, died that month of April, I was nine years old and her coffin sat in our living room surrounded by four enormous candles. Without our relatives' knowledge, I poured two drops of candle wax into the eyes of the alabaster virgin she held in her lap—drip and drip. Those two drops to cover the eyes of the figurine in consonance with *amabitxi*'s eyes were my way of saying goodbye.

When I was very young I confessed the name of the boy I liked to a friend. In the next village dance, she made sure to find a way to be kissed and fondled by him. I felt like a kitten with a petard exploding in its mouth. I perforated her disloyal eyes with needles in a photograph I found. To this day, if we coincide in the street, I don't see her and she doesn't see me.

About a month ago, with a key, I crushed the eyes of a little fluffy toy shark that hung from my car's rear view mirror. Crash, crash, little eyes *kaput.* It sounded like when you step on dry pasta tubes. This alter ego of M.'s can no longer see, can no longer dance along the road. He is exactly as he should be; he is just like me.

Those, among others, have been my methods of practicing *an eye for an eye.* Since I've had the bravery to confess such demented rites, it must be true that they've helped me sublimate the anguish of abandonment, the anger at betrayal, the despondency of impotence. Picking at the scabs of wounds and letting them dry in the air is a mark of overcoming difficult times; in this case, staunching the wounds means writing about them.

BIRDS, COLD AND BROKEN WINGS

It's been cold these past few days. Icicles hang from eaves and the frost crunches loud under my feet as I walk. The wind makes me lurch one side, then another. It's going to tear the gorse bushes from the roots; they're going to fly.

I take the hiking trail around Port d'Albret's marine lake. A section is populated by tamarinds. Together with willows, tamarinds are my favourite trees, because their hunchback tops looks like a misty green drizzle. In both trees, the branches are undecided, they go both up and down, bent double while trying to ascend (it happens to many of us). I rub some leaves between my palms, imprinting their nervations on my skin, I breathe their scent. I press a leaf between the pages of the book I carry in my backpack.

I'm seeing more birds than ever. They're finding it hard to find food, that's why they come so close to the path. In the grip of the freeze, they don't even have the will to get frightened. First a blackbird. A bit later, a thrush pecking on a snail; it hits the shell to get through and eat the entrails. It stares at me, impassive, and shows me its dappled chest. It doesn't run away because it must pursue its challenge (like I must do mine). Curlews in the estuary. Not a soul around.

Last spring a hungry robin would fly down to Karraspio all the time and cheekily sneak into M.'s car. He gave her bits of walnut.

'She looks like you,' he told me over the phone. 'She observes me so attentively, and is so peaceful.'

'It must be my totem. I sent her from Bilbao to watch over you.'

'Maybe: you're both the same colour, and she watches my bum when I undress to go into the water.'

Then he murmured an onomatopoeia ... tweet, tweet, tweet. I'd get wet just listening to him. I'd burn, bloom, come unglued.

M. brought me jay feathers from the forest. M. showed me the nest of a couple of hawks on the cliffs of Endai. M. returned a baby crow that had fallen off its nest to its mama crow. M. freed a seagull choking in a tangle of fishing tackle, cutting the line with his teeth. M.'s arms looked like wings to me when he lifted me in the air, and now that we each fly our separate routes along the low line of sky, cold paralyses my extremities. M. doesn't know about Janis. I'm not a little bird willing to eat crumbs out of M.'s hand.

A sign lights up high above the dunes. I climb up a concrete slope. Young people inside. I eat dinner here, for the first time since my arrival: mussels *Les Landes* style. When I get up to leave someone waves hello from a corner. I don't recognise her.

'How are the marigolds, still alive?'

Simone puts her beret on and we leave together. We could almost be mother and daughter.

'Where have you been? I never see you.'

She speaks to me as if we were friends.

'I'm writing a book.'

'Oh wow! What is it about?'

I tell her the title. I regret it as soon as I've said it, the conversation is about to turn surreal.

'Is it about magic? Fortune tellers' crystal balls are eyes, right?'

I let out a disgruntled snort. She can't be serious, is she?

'Let's say it's a *self-imitation*.'

'*A, bon!* It's hardly noticeable ... just because you mention it now, otherwise...'

But she gets nervous and starts talking about camera lenses,

Christmas globes, bubbles... an incredible number of free associations. Useful ideas for my book. I should note them down. When we arrive at my place she plants a soft kiss on my lips. Afterwards I see the glow of her cigarette move and disappear through the bushes.

I had five missed calls on my phone: three from my father and two from a number with a Bizkaian prefix. Another call. My uncle.

'Jesus, where have you been?'

He starts to scold me, telling me off for not being at hand when I'm needed. He's out of his mind. He can't understand my going away from home for so long, even less so leaving my son behind. And the two of them, my two old men.

'Your father fell on the street. An ambulance took him away.'

'Who's with him?'

'Who do you think? No one! It's hard enough for me to deal with myself.'

Grumblingly, I put some clothes and my notebook in a bag, and head out to Galdakao hospital. I take Janis along too, although I know Simone would look after her if I asked.

I go through almost an entire kitchen roll in the journey, so profuse are my tears and need to blow my nose. Cellulose is so useful, a companionable soft hand belonging to no one. Crying serves as an outlet for my rage and self-pity. It wouldn't be hard to have a crash, I think, on the motorway, pretend that sleep took over me. But no, my father expects me. And I'll hug my son the day after tomorrow. He's only fifteen.

I listen to the radio as I drive. Great news today, October 20th: the ETA put down their arms for good.

I arrive in the hospital at 2am. *Aita* broke an arm, but the real worry is a brain injury. He bled out of his ears and has to be closely monitored to make sure there is no internal haemorrhaging. He

88

snores placidly, thanks to the painkillers. I hate my old man's snoring (what don't I hate, sometimes). Now it's time to repress that feeling.

She's arrived, She Who Can Do Everything—as someone, I can't recall who, once said. Nurse, secretary, chauffeur and cook twenty-four hours a day. I remember something George Eliot once wrote as I kiss *aita* on the forehead: 'A woman's happiness is to be made as cakes are, by a fixed recipe.' I've never been a melodious sparrow in the wheat fields, a cicada, but it annoys the shit out of me to have to look after someone precisely now, when my wing is broken, even if my bones are all in one piece.

MONOPHTALMIA AND EVERYDAY LIFE

Work regulations don't include any restrictions regarding one-eyed people; as long as they prove their ability, they can have any career they want.

Polyphemus. King Christian IV of Denmark. Ana de Mendoza, Princess of Eboli (she lost her eye in a fencing exercise, or as a consequence of syphilitic keratitis, depending on the sources). Grigory Aleksandrovich, Count of Potemkin. Hannibal Barca, Quintus Sertorius, Wenceslaus II King of Bohemia, Lord Horatio Nelson and Blas de Lezo (all lost theirs in battles). Luís de Camões, author of the epic poem *The Lusiads*. The physicist Nicolas-Jacques Conté (a hydrogen explosion while carrying out an experiment). Marconi (road accident). The actors Peter Falk and Rex Harrison. The cinema directors Raoul Walsh and John Ford (a hare leaped into the road while the first was location-hunting for one of his movies; things are not so clear as regards the second: evil tongues said that he just had a collection of eye patches he liked to use, it was all pure snobbery on his part). The musician Sammy Davis Jr. The Israeli Prime Minister Moshe Dayan. The models for some works of art (for example, Picasso's *La vieja*, or the French School's 1566 *The One-Eyed Flautist*). Captain Hook. Some zombies. María de Villota, the Formula 1 pilot (lost it in a race). The bullfighter Padilla (a bull took it out). Daryl Hannah in *Kill Bill*. Helen Parker, Haar, Solidus Snake and Demoman; video game characters. Tuerta de Luxe, a one-eyed hooker that advertises on Facebook.

Having only one eye is a deficit, there for anyone to see

(apologies for the too-easy play on words, I couldn't resist). That's why if you have one eye, you have to keep it on the prize (and this expression too, it's just too appropriate to miss).

In the Middle Ages it was a commonly held opinion that the senses were the entryway to any kind of knowledge. There were high-level discussions to elucidate who were more wretched, deaf or blind people. As regards the one-eyed, they weren't thought to be valueless people, but they weren't considered completely normal either (and according to superstition, they were bearers of bad luck). Be that as it may, depending on the case and after a period of adaptation, one-eyed people can lead normal lives. After overcoming some obstacles that can result from our physical limitation, that is.

For example, parking. To open the garage door, descend two floors in the semi-darkness without scraping against the many columns and then complete manoeuvres with ease in order to park one's car in one's spot without scratching the paintwork, is not something that one achieves from one day to the next. Calculating distances is quite the thing, as we see half a metre where there is one. Hence the law that, until it's recent amendment, forced one-eyed people to renew our driving licences every two years.

Another thing, pouring liquids. Although etiquette and good manners censor this, our trick is to feel the glass with the neck of the bottle to make sure the wine falls inside it; if we don't, ninety nine percent of the time the first glug will land on the tablecloth.

For this reason, it's difficult for us to play *pala*, the Basque version of tennis, and when we descend rocky terrains we have to crouch down and feel the stones to make sure our feet go where they should. And obviously, 3D films don't bring us the pleasure and delight that leads other audiences to applause.

Or it may be the case that physical limitations evolve into psychological ones. On the one hand, as it's been established, and because psychomotricity is hampered by reduced overall vision, a person's character comes into play: whether they shrink in the face of difficulties or if they like facing up to challenges. On the other, although being one-eyed and being cross-eyed are not the same thing, if the one-eyed person becomes cross-eyed, don't be surprised if their self-esteem is somewhat impaired.

Have you ever been in front of someone with a glass eye? Or in front of someone who has a small defect in their eye, even? A burst blood vessel, slight strabismus. People get nervous. They always talk to you looking at your eye; it's unintentional, the eye always beckons the eye. And if it's you who talks to someone over there, that person will turn their head, in doubt as to whether you're talking to them or someone else.

People with a glass eye can't focus both of their eyes on the same point.

TO SHARPEN, TO POLISH

There was a letter from the Basque Government in my letter box. They awarded the Euskadi Prize to *Errepidea*, a book of mine (the main character is a thirteen-year-old girl; she and a number of birds are the narrators. M. provided every bit of knowledge about them, as well as all the details about the constellations). The news barely touched me. All I felt was an overwhelming desire to tell M.

No time to breathe: I shower, change clothes, eat something, attend to Janis and return to hospital in a rush.

In the hours I spend watching over my father, I make some notes on these pages. I can't do more than that. Kandinsky *dixit*: 'There is no must in art, because art is free.' Hahahaha.

After five days they release us, once *aita*'s arrhythmia is under control. The return home is tremendous. My uncle is not at his best, and *aita* needs to stay in bed (his arm is in a plaster cast and half his face is bruised). It's the second time he falls this year and the damage is increasingly disastrous. We argue because they don't want to hire anyone to look after them. *Aita* flies off the handle any time I suggest anything. We are like a knife and a sharpening stone.

When I'm at my parents' I put on one of my mother's old tracksuits to do the housework more comfortably. This works against me because dressed like that I look more like her, and I'm irritated by the unease this causes me—I am her daughter, so I fear acting like her and taking on the penitence of looking after my dad and uncle (*ama* neglected her health in the chokehold of

93

sacrifice, in her effort to watch over my grandparents and their chronic illnesses). When I hurry from kitchen to bedroom, up and down the corridor, to empty his bedpan, to feed him his pills, to change his sheets or rub cream on his bald head, it's rancour that drives me, not affection. Even though I am the best nurse in the world (that's what *aita* tells all visitors), I don't shower him with smiles, or words of encouragement. Apart from a polite kiss here and there, I show him little affection.

I can't stand *aita*'s old age. I'm repulsed by his stupefied look, his slowness, the ease with which he inhabits that indefinable space between sanity and indolence. We get on, in general, and he's proud of me, but his eyes sparkle with joy every time he sees me with some cleaning product or a broom at hand, servicing him (making him feel secure). I can't stand it. He bosses me around, demanding this or that without letting me finish what I'm doing. It drives me up the wall, his need to always feel superior: the day he dies he'll demand we switch the heating off or turn the key in the lock from his coffin.

He's not like that because he chooses to. He is controlled by rage: old age means resignation. One day, on the verge of foaming at the mouth, he shouted at me: 'I'm angry! Because I'm always in a bad mood!' I felt pity for him, it sounded like the sorrowful confession of a sick man who suffers an incurable disease.

What would he do without me? He knows the answer.

I too know that he is afraid of losing his autonomy, and that he's terrified of death. I know that he needs affectionate support, but his beastly manners, his urge to prod me, push me away. I get angry because the time I dedicate to my father is a direct subtraction from my peace.

Subtracting from my peace and adding toxic addends to my character are one and the same thing. I shout at him with old, repressed resentment.

'I'm not going to be the price of your well-being, do you hear? Not I.'

He shuts up. Verbalising my anger refreshes my mouth, however. Sharp tongue, polished thought.

I finish things and leave. I leave because he wants me there, stuck to him. He didn't expect this selfish daughter after more than eighty years on the planet. He sits on the bed, looking down, pinching his nappy. Don't be shocked: my dad is a tough guy, he doesn't awaken pity.

Or should we forbid ourselves rage?

As soon as I enter the lift I imagine her pleading with me: 'Look after *aita*, do it for me.' I answer in silence. 'Of course I will, *ama*, for you. Who else would I do that for?' The sting of conscience is persistent.

In the Club of Retirees they give me the number of a young man who looks after elderly people. We talk and agree: from next week on he'll take over the day-to-day of my old man.

Losing my temper with my father spurs me on.

I am very nervous, can't stop for a second. When I was cleaning up in *aita*'s house I found a box full of photographs at the top of a wardrobe. I went through them methodically, like a seamstress going through remnants spread all over her workshop floor deciding which ones she'll use and which she'll throw away. There were some photos of me in the mix, loose cells from a biographical organism.

I know and I don't know how time has passed until this moment: the photos only help me understand that in part. In any case, there was one among all of them that consoled me: a young girl, pen in hand, looking at a piece of paper with the eyes of someone who sees something for the first time. I realise that the moment the picture captures is the root of all of memory—call it life, call it fiction.

Seeing my son gives me strength. I missed him terribly during my 'exile'. His mother's attitude towards him must have seemed so pathetic to him. I feel guilty not being able to hold it together for him.

'Your grandfather is a *troll*,' I told him a couple of nights ago in a Chinese restaurant in Santutxu.

His favourite sentence (my favourite sentence) showed me that he still understands me.

'Don't worry, *amatxu*.'

So what if he's like that, such a mature teenager. He also knows how to ignore everything when things are fine. He told me:

'You'll find someone who'll love you the way you need to be loved.'

A sentence worthy of applause. He thinks I expect something different. I thought so too. He's too young to understand that, at the end of the day, we don't change that much.

These few days back in the village have strengthened me. I am bound to the pebbled streets, to the old shops and bars, to the *bidegorri* trail and to the port like any other aspect of the landscape: I belong to this place.

The Southerly is blowing. Even if tiredness is killing my eyes, I discern, from Santa Katalina Lighthouse, *un ray vert* beyond Arzabal Point, in the distant white shores, awaiting my return.

A DROP OF POISON

'I want to see you.'

'…I'm half asleep.'

'Don't lie, your balcony light is still on. I'm coming up.'

I hear M. coming up the stairs two at a time. Although I'm conscious of the risk opening the door implies, the painful deficit of not having seen M. in so long wins. Eyes get thirsty too.

I don't hug him, he doesn't hug me. An uncomfortable silence occupies the space of compliments. Here's M., with his defenceless look. That's the danger of M. for me, that look that makes me want to be his refuge.

'Everyday, when I go to the bakery or to the port, I pass by your house and think "Where is Meibi? How is she?" I've come to tell you, I want you to know.'

I press my lips together. He reads the disapproval in my gesture: the rules of the game have changed. He speaks directly into my eyes.

'That day on the beach, when we spoke for the first time, you were there because *you* had to be there.'

A drop of poison for the parched. It's not fair.

'I miss you,' he adds.

'I do too, but what does that mean.'

Nostalgia won't patch over the cracks of agony of the last few months. He can't use an alternative for that fucking line I've never heard from his lips ('I love you.' Is it really that hard to say? In any case I'd rather not hear it than hearing a lukewarm 'I love you my way').

I don't know what he expects. Sometimes we seek an anchor, we want a ballast, we don't really know why. I'll never know what it is that drags M. towards me; if it's love, pleasure, or gratitude. Or the sum total of all.

'Don't suffer so much,' I say, 'you and I know how to have a bad time, we've done it before.'

It would have been easy to give in to temptation and show greater resistance to test his sincerity. But I find it an absurd tactic, unless you're someone who enjoys playing a double game.

Disappointment shows in M.'s cheeks.

'You don't believe in fate, I know that. But we have to talk,' he insists.

'Tomorrow, on the beach.'

Clarifying note. In this period joblessness rates have increased. The crisis the media won't stop banging on about makes people clench their fists tight so as not to lose a single penny, while many others gather around the backs of supermarkets to retrieve discarded food from their rubbish containers. According to NGOs, there are no appropriate resources, not even close, to attend to the lines of people begging for help. Some families have had to turn to grandparents because their pensions are the only source of income.

The epicentre of the crisis is a political fiction, a toxic bubble programmed by financial institutions. Has capital ever been willing to lose control? They can go fuck themselves.

I don't suddenly bring this up in a fit of social engagement that demands that I denounce this polluted society (which would be pure demagoguery, given my lifestyle), but because I am ashamed by the fact that the unmovable centre of this work is my desire, day in and day out. In a way, I feel dirty for being so miserable. Will you accept my apologies? If your answer is no, don't turn over the page. Tell me to fuck off.

TROMPE L'OEIL

A residue of summer at the end of October. Clear skies. Low tide.

We reach the island at my pace. I harbour important thoughts as I swim next to M.: 'I haven't shaved my legs, I'm so pale, I need a new swimsuit.'

There are cormorants on the rocks.

We do it quickly. When we finish, a kiss on my left shoulder, same as always. And new words: 'My Meibi.'

I didn't feel any emotion. I don't know where the funereal tone of my moans has gone. I didn't sense a need to say anything, not for fear that a tender word would get trapped in my throat, like before, but because words get in the way when you just want to validate a simple act.

M. didn't say he loves me, or how much (are quantity and intensity concepts that can be expressed, anyway?). M. won't give the topical, magical sentence a chance to escape: he wants to carry it in his marrow, or not at all.

I remember the encounter as if I'd watched it through a camera that focussed on me in duplicate, inside the scene and outside it at the same time. I could resume it into a sequence of images. And when I say images I don't strictly mean contents we capture through our sight: aren't images conjured by touch, hearing or smell, or the mental images collaged by the sum of all of the above—synesthetic imagery—more ineradicable?

One: The woman turns her face up. A flock of pigeons darkens the sky. The woman draws a straight line (the trajectory of rain drops, a ray of light, the line of the fisherman who searches for his soul in the mouths of fish, a string instrument's chord, any pure colour). The retina has memories. The woman turns around her axis, an arm extended as if to swipe the landscape.

Two: The saliva of waves, the sails of jellyfish, a wooden word adrift, ampoules of light among the seaweed.

What is there in a droplet? Pronouns: you and I, not quite we.

In that fragile mirror, an invitation to the abyss.

The woman's hands are cold. The man takes them, covers them with his.

Three: The autumn awards her what the summer never did: staples to hold back her tears.

This is the situation in a crevice at the island: feet firm on a rock covered in lichen, hands against a rock wall, the white dance of breasts released from a swimsuit. The man ejaculates. Midday's high sun lights up their lips like gin lip-gloss. They swim back to the shore. The man's acrid breath is a chandelier that brightens the water ditches.

Four: The woman now knows that the beach is a background. *Love me, love me, love me,* say her footsteps as they mark the sand.

It'll all stay behind the glass after the rains.

Like taxis that dwell in the peripheries, they'll both retreat to the voice of mist.

What they gave each other will feel like the red roof of a fairytale.

Five: And the point – the confluence of all image-icons, the first squeal of any letter. You, in the distance.

As it's well known, images can fool our sight, making us believe that what *is* isn't, or is something else. There is a modality of decorative painting used throughout the ages that consists in the replication of architectural elements—doors, arches or windows—or inanimate or animate objects—animals, trees or fountains—or, also, ornamental objects—paintings, curtains or vases. This technique, called *trompe l'oeil* in French or *trampantojo* in Spanish, highlights the idea of trickery. The corresponding word in *Euskara* to express this trick that fools the eye, however, is *miragune*, which also means mirage or optical illusion. Although it could be said that in terms of terminological specificity it's insufficient, I think it's an ideal word to indicate fascination. Truly, mirages, hallucinations, tricks, are mere images. Simple, hollow, void.

THE EYES OF MY DEAD

I can stay here for All Saints Day. 'Dust you are and to dust you shall return,' the priest used to tell us while, with his thumb, he marked our foreheads with a cross. Maybe T.S. Eliot's line 'I will show you fear in a handful of dust' has something to do with this. When my *aitita* the sacristan explained to me that he made the liturgical ashes himself burning branches of blessed laurels, the whole mystery of the thing dissipated for me.

My body boils. I lean my hands on the pantheon. They burn as if I'd rested them on kitchen burners. I remove withered bunches of flowers and scrape the lichen off with a file (and again, who is in charge of this business of keeping our dead's last resting place neat?).

The vaporous light of the cemetery lamps reminds me of the stove in our old kitchen. The women would lift the burner's lids with a hook and throw in potato peels, kindling and scraps of food. The flames would almost touch their rough hands that smelt of beans, bleach, cheap cologne and medication. They raised me between them: *ama, amuma, tia, amabitxi*. If I follow on my ancestors' example, my death won't be a memorable event, but a discreet end after a long sequence of pitiful sorrows.

Ama would draw a cross in the header of every letter she wrote; whether it was for my father at sea, or for my aunt in America. Thanks to that superstition she'd trust her will and felt freed from ever saying the wrong word. I learnt the art of prudence from her.

Amuma never spoke unless she had something to say. She preferred attending to her sewing, knitting, or mending, and keeping her thoughts to herself. She spent five years in bed, paralysed by ankylosis, incapable of even turning over on one side. She taught me the power of silence.

My *tia* (*amuma*'s unmarried sister, whom *amuma* took in when a bomb destroyed the family farmstead during the war) would shake her head every time I grumbled about something. With her, I learnt to appreciate rectitude. She'd wake up every morning to make me breakfast before I went to school. She would also prepare a bowl of boiled water with a bit of salt and balls of cotton wool, to wash my eyes. We slept together. I'd hear her scratch herself, or pinch her body furiously. 'Nothing, *umea*, go to sleep.' One morning, when we were together in the kitchen, a stream of blood flowed from under her skirt. I didn't understand where that blood spreading over the kitchen tiles came from, that chocolate-coloured blood, at breakfast time no less. Have you ever heard about vulval cancer?

I met *amabitxi*, my godmother sick with pleurisy, already bedbound. She would read me the feats of martyrs and saints every afternoon when I came back from school. She promised I'd have the ring on her finger, the one with the purple stone, when she was no longer there. She gave me lessons on common courtesy, when to say *por favor, gracias, usted*, and to whom.

I grew up surrounded by old ladies. I owe every 'but' to them; to the curious, fierce, penetrating, tender, never indifferent, complimentary, weary and loving looks of my dead. Even though the worms must have long been done with them, their eyes have never left me. Their legacy bears no value for anyone, except for me; just like these reflections have no other objective but to accompany me: paper pulp they are and paper pulp they shall become.

On one occasion I read the definition of viscose in a clothes shop. I was surprised to see that paper pulp is the raw material with which viscose is made. It seems that paper pulp allows other substances to move like silk when it's added to them. In a similar way, these thoughts will make my nostalgia feel lighter.

Regarding childhood nostalgia, experts say that it's something like a first layer of repressed fury. Years might come and go, but behaviours acquired in childhood persist: like chilblains, they disappear but have a tendency to re-emerge. Let's therefore say that all learning has its reverses, which are not quite as shiny and neat as medals or lottery tickets.

For example, the reverse of prudence is the inability to develop the guts to stand up to someone who raises their voice. Diplomacy, therefore, has its ignominious side.

The variants of silence are so many that, every now and then, what we don't say, what we half say and what we say in secret can bring us as much benefit as terror.

Similarly, sentences such as 'Come on, chin up, it's nothing' and other ones like it can be false expressions of rectitude. Saying amen is an easily affordable placebo that serves to substitute our instinct to protest.

And the reverse of courtesy is hypocrisy. Because it's so difficult to establish where one ends and the other one begins, you learn to skate on the rings of ambiguity—so graceful and innocent.

I am thankful for the good lessons of the women in our house, and revise their so-so ones. The only serious imputable charge I can accuse them of is this: their inability to teach me to say no. Let us say that my mother's milk, together with her many vitamins, planted the seeds of the *yesofcourse* bloom in my tongue. The flowers that eventually bloom from those seeds are made of straw, and tear up the flesh of your mouth if you try to remove them.

The women in my family didn't want to live alone, didn't seek changes, they were in no doubt as to their objectives. However, I can't ascertain that they never caught sight of a different door, or that they never felt the need to cross it. Thankfully, it is not my intention to investigate their secrets, virtues, furies, defects, fears, envies and frustrations. I have no intention of distorting them, like I'm doing with mine.

Weaknesses:
1. *Too many ecclesiastical words: sacristan, bless, martyrs, cross, pantheon…*
2. *The women I refer to may appear to be idealised. Write a more conscious critique of abnegation (the description of the negative aspects is too subtle).*
3. *If I have no intention of perpetuating tradition, what is my real message regarding these two previous points?*
4. *The island scene (previous chapter) and the scene in the cemetery clash against one another.*

Leave them as they are. In the end, that's how things happened. I often go to one place as much as the other, sometimes in the same day too.

THE GLASS EYE, A TOPIC

Typing 'crystal eye' in the search engine throws back lots of references, from classical examples to contemporary ones, a multitude of glass eyes. But, what are those entities flickering in the Internet universe? (Let us leave cinema aside, particularly the terror genre and the amusement sadistic torturers derive from injuring their victims' eyes.)

Overall, glass eyes are a metaphor, part of the legacy of the history of literature, an image that's turned into a topic. Here are some cases:

Shakespeare mentions them in 'Sonnet 46'. Crystal eyes (in other words, pure eyes) are the characteristic *par excellence* of the damsel, a lady's attribute of spiritual beauty. Bartholomew Griffin does something similar when he compares eyes with stars: *…the purest, crystal eye hath seen. / Her eyes, the brightest stars…*

In other cases, crystal eyes are stars, directly, like in this verse by Robert Service: *That crystal eye that raked the sky…*

Besides being associated to stars, glass eyes are often linked to water too, despite the resulting, rather pathetic: *Your waves are made of glass, the waves of your eyes, the waves of your glass eyes…* (Pee Wee). Owing to the similarity between glass and water, glass eyes can express sadness, as well as the aforementioned honesty. Thus, for Henry King, the author of a 1669 poem set to music two hundred years later by the composer Edward Elgar, they were eyes that cried: *Dry those fair, those crystal eyes…*

But as regards this *récit*, the glass eye is the point from which my ramblings radiate, the repetitive element that structures the feeble syntax of this narrative. Discordances aside, the different chapters lead into the eye or flow out of the eye. Therefore, and thanks to the generosity of semantics, call it pearl, marble, pebble, little egg, coral, bead, star, bubble, ball, globule, prosthesis or whatever you like, my glass eye is my own private topic, and I have every right to it.

I print out the score for the Elgar song and stick it on the cover of my notebook. It looks so elegant. I could have put a postcard of the dunes there instead. Or a photo of my 'shining star' (I'm talking about my eye, not M.). Or a mirror.

The score gives it a nineteenth century feel, a pity. Because this is a modern text. Or is it? It's slightly anachronistic, this endless going over the telling of a loss, isn't it? It'd be so much better to mouth an indifferent 'So what?' turn around and put an end to this story for once and fucking all. But no: I am making a tireless effort to show that even though I was used to being She Who Waits (those who love, wait, they say), my eyes were highly sensitive, yes, but never passive.

ONE STAR

I haven't seen M. after what happened in the island (we didn't make the slightest effort to meet up). Although I keep analysing myself, I've calmed down. Before, I had no peace, I'd unravel every word we said to one another, every gesture and every look. I was imprisoned by an unreachable aim: the thirst for oneness.

I told him plainly: 'I'm not getting back together with you.'

I came to my garden. It's abandoned. It's been a long time since anyone set foot here and the plants have grown awkwardly. During my absence the wind has broken some planters. When I see all the withered flowers my eyes seek marigolds. Yes, a couple, belated ones, poor things. The miniature pumpkins have rotted on the earth. When they bloom, the orange flowers of the pumpkin look like birds' beaks; later on they shrink and whiten, shaping into spongy flames. In summer nights you can hear the frogs' song. When I came in today, the birds didn't all fly off at the same time like they usually do.

The plot is in the half-light. There are shaded corners where moss swallows the light, and sunny patches the cats stretch out on. The apple trees are on one side, and on the wall closest to them, an expanse of broad-leaved red ivy. On the other side, the pear trees and the naked vine. It's impossible to tell where the bougainvilleas, the azaleas, the petunias, the carnations are now.

There's a little stone house in a corner, it's very old. An eavestrough carries rainwater from the roof to a reservoir.

Because it's the dampest area of the garden, the lemon tree, holly and lavender grow strong there. There is a palm tree by the house too, and on its feet, rose bushes planted around a stone railing. I used to put my writing table there. I'd get up often to water the plants or remove dry leaves. Such actions, in their simplicity, felt like brief conversations ('How are you, *txiki*? Here I am, paying attention to you'). The spotted geraniums and the purple hydrangea were the most grateful. And me too, because pottering around the garden was almost always a recourse that soothed my distress at not being able to fill the pages. Often, this has been the refuge where I come to get over the bad times. Oh, Emily Dickinson, always so wise. *When I believe the garden / mortal shall not see— / pick by faith its blossom / and avoid its bee, / I can spare this summer, unreluctantly.* If our inner garden is not tilled with seeds that please us, forget about it. Like pumpkin flowers, our hours go by distended sometimes, sometimes contracted, because life is a concatenation of goodbyes, reiterations of pain, and in-between, periods of love.

This place is not a paradise lost (for it is here now), it is not a bucolic landscape (planting the hibiscus and getting rid of weeds cost me sweat), it is not my *sancta sanctorum* (whatever transpires here is of this world), it's not a club (the door is open to those who'd come through). Here I've glimpsed those fleeting moments that pin us to life—a butterfly hiding in the bosom of a calla lily or a magpie's beak splitting a live worm in two. In this place I have paid attention to detail, I have weighted the reasons for each choice, and enjoyed the process according to my rules: in this place, I have written.

Is that so important?

I've sought looseness of rhythm, originality of structure, the true union of time and space; I've outlined thoughts and feelings; I've lassoed words from conversations with friends; I've questioned what I do and what I achieved in doing it at every turn. To write is not to assemble Meccanos of sentences but to square up to the most intimate whirlwinds, the harmonious as much as the distorted ones. It's an unsettling endeavour, and we must ask our stomach for permission to carry it out. It can't always be done, and it isn't easy, or free. We must be strong to accept the fate of what spurts and grows inside our writing.

Mary Annette Beauchamp von Arnim lived in a remote farm in Pomerania with her three daughters, as she wrote in her novel *Elizabeth and her German Garden*. With irony and sensitivity, and through her love of tending to trees and plants, she expressed her rebellion against social mores: *The whole of this radiant Easter day I have spent out of doors, sitting at first among the windflowers and celandines […] and the afternoon was so hot that we lay a long time on the turf, blinking up through the leafless branches of the silver birches […] It makes one very humble to see oneself surrounded by such a wealth of beauty and perfection anonymously lavished, and to think of the infinite meanness of our own grudging charities […] I do sincerely trust that the benediction that is always awaiting me in my garden may by degrees be more deserved, and that I may grow in grace, and patience, and cheerfulness, just like the happy flowers I so much love.* Looking after flowers is no flimsy pastime.

The garden has a touch of the wild in that tangled climbing jasmine, in the invasive clover, in the quenchless nettle; something rational about the lines of peas, green beans and pepper plants; something dreamy about the reddish leaves of the climbers; something protective about the mint, the incense, the basil plants; and mystery under the fallen leaves the rake never stirs. I've attached to this garden meanings of my convenience. That's why it's my refuge.

Will you look at this: a glass eye looking at me from above. Thank you so much, Edith Matilda Thomas: *Apple-green west and an orange bar, and the crystal eye of a lone, one star.* It blinks, one eye winking at another. A topic on another topic. Message received:

110

look after the earth, wipe the mirror clean. Garden and writing are, for me, parallel refuges: *locus (amoenus) conclusus et inconclusus.*

I come to the garden for Janis. I open the cage and the bird melts into the November sky. Night won't interrupt her flight-path.

THE GOOD THING ABOUT GOOD TIMING

'Mitxu! Give me a hug!'

G. is affectionate even when she's telling you off.

'You look like a beggar. I don't want to see you like this. Let's go to the hairdresser's. When did you last have your roots done? You weren't born to be a hermit, my darling. Where have you been hiding, in the desert?'

'More or less…' I whimper, moved by the rescue effort.

We buy a jacket each. I wouldn't have chosen anything if she hadn't pushed me, I don't like clothes shopping.

'See, ten years younger in one afternoon. All we need now is some lingerie.'

We walk to *Eskalope* arm in arm. We choose bras and knickers, pretty ones. We say goodbye with a couple of kisses.

'See you soon, *laztana*. I look forward to hearing you say that you found something, and not lost it, all right…?'

My friend is so smart.

I used to do crazy things with lingerie in the M. days. I would buy pieces that I've worn only once. They weren't expensive on their own but, once (on one occasion?), they added up to more than three hundred euro.

I don't care about your judgement, what you think about me or this thing I'm writing. Transparent fabrics, arseless knickers and tights and suspenders are the anteroom of pleasure that live inside my drawers and the guarantee of desire in my imagination. Although I'm a bit dull when it comes to *striptease*, I can give and receive pleasure until all oxygen is sucked out of the room.

I find *aita* sitting on an armchair, talking to a photo of *ama*. He's better.

'I'll call you to let you know that I've arrived in one piece.'

He's going to be in a bad mood when I leave, I know it. I give him a hug.

'OK,' he says. 'Careful on the road.'

I relax when I see the nice man everyone sees in my dad.

My uncle brings me a daily desktop calendar from his room.

'You like to read other sorts of things, but there are some beautiful things in here too.'

He's in the habit of reading the daily page, front and back: sunrise and sunset times, moonrise and moonset times, fasting days, quotes from famous people and refrains from all over the world, the name of each day's saint, animal customs, mini myths and fairytales, health recommendations, prayers, household tips and all sorts of quirky things. Today, November 4th, I come across a quote by Helen Keller: *Never bend your head. Always hold it high. Look the world straight in the eye.*

'You know who she was, do you?' he asks. 'She was deaf and blind from childhood, but, what a woman!'

Trapped within the walls of silence and darkness, she learnt to listen and speak with her hands. To write too, and write she did. Unless I'm mistaken, it was her who said, apropos of life, that it's either a daring adventure, or nothing at all.

I visited my dead ones and left my little old men under watch. I return to my borrowed home.

SOUVENIRS FROM LEKEITIO

Simone's shop is closed when I go by around midday. I drop a box of pastries and a selection of postcards through her letterbox.

After lunch, I send Rémy a message: 'I still owe you a drink.' Soon we'll sample another white, *txakoli* from Mendexa.

Around mid-afternoon there's a knock on the door, a rare occurrence. It's a messenger with a package: *Attention, madame, c'est fragile*. I sign the yellow receipt, intrigued by the parcel's contents. No promise could be more precious to me than that collection of seeds of plants and flowers, cuttings and grafts wrapped in tin foil. They come with a note in M.'s hand: 'Waiting for Meibi.'

I write this fragment in bed, watching the man that sleeps by my side. I liked the feel of his moustache and the kisses he planted on my eyes; even more I liked the way he murmured French words in my ear. Rémy is a man that I could love. Rémy too.

Soon I won't need this house.

STILL LIFE

Simone and I have a good time together. We went to Baiona yesterday, to watch an exhibition of still lifes from across the ages—classical, modern.

Were I to compose a still life, what (or who) would be its central element?

Everything that is portrayed in paintings is dead, or is about to turn. Is it going to go to waste? No life can come out of dead matter. Or yes, sometimes it does. Sometimes something is born; of rotten seeds, for example.

As for what can be born out of a dead love, you are holding it in your hands. Some things are neither lost in vain, nor gone to waste.

Similarly, a painting has been born out of this poem. Herewith the chain of creation that brings forth creation.

Light doesn't come from a single source, from a corner, from high up.

Light radiates from the very figures in the painting.

A tablecloth with lace detail gives the table the feel of an altar.

Rimbaud once said: 'There is a God who laughs at the damask cloths

of the altars, at the incense… who falls asleep in the lullaby of Hosannas…'

Roses fall from a crystal vase onto a tray of oysters.

The petals mingle with the harsh grey shells and the wet yellow flesh.

A seashell decorates a cake.

Eggs fill a nest, fungi fill a basket, a salmon fills a net.

Watermelon, grapes, pomegranates, pears, cherries in the mirror, in its reflection.

Ripeness. Softness. Taste.

The snail crawls over the pink-hued wooden body of a lute.

The caterpillar chews on a tulip's corolla and the ant shoulders a breadcrumb.

Fingerprints on a knife's blade.

The butterfly pauses on the rim of a wine glass.

Wine flows from another, knocked-over glass. The spill stains the tablecloth.

A just blown-out candle smokes.

Fragility. Brevity. Transience.

In the painting's chiaroscuro, my eye senses an atmosphere of wellbeing.

The scene is like a catalogue of pleasures.

It represents a concern for food.

It represents a lifestyle.

It represents the generosity of nature.

It represents humans' power over it.

There is also a pocket watch with a blue silk ribbon.

Tick-tock. *Memento mori*. Remember that you are mortal.

It also represents the artist's concern with the human condition.

The ensemble – the solidity of the domestic artifacts, the beauty of the creatures,

the skin of the fruits, the almost-palpable blast of aromas – soothes my eye.

The perfection of that copy of reality is one side of the coin.

The ensemble – the stillness of the trousseau and the dead animals, the insects'
     fervour,

the fruit beginning to rot, the almost-palpable blast of aromas – perturbs my eye.

A disquieting emotional subtext is the other side of the coin.

Bravo. *Juste milieu*: the perfect equilibrium of a two-sided piece.

The symbolism of the piece is moralising.

It offers a double perspective on the world.

Pleasures and losses. Excesses and wants.

Light and shadows influence one another.

A book. Science. A score. Art. A broken clay figurine, lame. Leisure.

It's a placid nature. Its tranquility is false.

It's a necropolis, this still life.

Formula. *Vanitas vanitatum omnia vanitas*. Vanity of vanities, all is vanity.

It notes the magnificence of life and remembers the certainty of death.

116

There is a what, a why, a what for, and a how. There is a process.

The process links botany, zoology, architecture and religion.

Is the painting finished? Colour, texture, harmony, composition, perspective.

Is the eye complete? Eyelid, eyelash, sclerotic, iris, pupil.

Is the idea concrete? Allegory, reason, dream, emotion, reflection.

Balance. Gravitas. Weighty enough to be considered a work of art.

I touch the scarf on my neck. It has a motif of birds and flowers

that matches the colours in the painting.

I look at my shoes. They have a silver buckle,

its glint is also in the painting.

I put my hands inside my coat. It has pockets,

a certain depth, like the background in the painting.

The background is a subtle landscape with columns, an idealised garden.

Spectacles. *Trompe l'oeil*. A trick of the eye, *trampantojo*.

What is outside the painting? What season is it? Where?

Garlands like white-teared heliotropes, Christmas.

Take a step, then another, take a step, then another.

Write one letter down, write another, write one letter down, write another.

Walk on until the beach is here. The landscape changes my eye.

Piles of blood-red algae like giant, drowned hedgehogs.

Yourcenar said: 'Death, at most, is the innocent worm of a gorgeous fruit.'

The light, a brush. The shadow, a palette. The word, my moving eye.

The shadow draws the figures in the world.

The shadow precludes access to all details.

BOLT OR AXLE

Who misses the hard times? Wounded wings, even when they heal, won't soar to the heights of times past.

Were I to lose someone (or something) that I love, would I act as timidly, as stupidly, as meekly again? I've been just as timorous as many others, to my regret. Or not: thank fuck we're weak (ten points, Anari, for *eskerrak ahulak garen,* what a song). M. used to say that to throw oneself into matters of the heart too eagerly is the road to perdition, that we can't allow ourselves to love to the point of sickness. He's ahead of me in that regard.

He confirmed what I already knew: the worm of *it's over* begins to eat away at love as soon as it germinates. And yes, every goodbye is an enucleation. And every surgery, from an appendicitis extraction to a hara-kiri, has its interesting side: getting rid of a sickly organ is a bit like correcting a bad habit (how many times did I hide my anger, for example. Having spent a sleepless, furious night ruminating on M.'s behaviour, the morning after I'd welcome him with a sweet smile; and if, on rare occasions, I welcomed him with a scowl, his attitude would immediately turn my mood around. I'd behave like one of those thick balls of dust that roll from corner to corner in filthy houses. Don't criticise me, I'm better than anyone at berating myself). One must allow time to pass for emotional bruises to fade away.

It's undeniable that love makes the horrendous seem gorgeous and glosses over defects. We glow in the company of our beloved, but love can defeat and break us if we don't find it or if we lose it. And that can carry an additional cost: an increased loss of dignity. These are some of the risks those who love undertake.

They lead us to believe that love and happiness go hand in hand, and that's how it sometimes is. Doubtlessly, however, love and pain go together more often: love fails when too much is asked of it.

You'll tell me that love is only one of the bolts in the machine that each one of us is, and not the axle. I'll tell you that, bolt or axle, it's the centripetal force that propels my lines nine times out of ten. You'll tell me that love is a temporal union—only in some cases long-lasting. And that, ultimately, we are ruled by percentages of dopamine and oxytocin. I'll tell you, yes, you're right, we each make love up as we go along: no two eyes are the same, just like no two people are the same.

IF, IF, IF...

As regards the men I've loved, here's the following résumé: I gave one what we always give when we're twenty, the naiveté of the world *forever*; I gave my husband my willingness to be defined by him during my best years, and our son; that other guy, I gave him a few unforgettable, secret hours; to M., the open air and everything these pages can and cannot contain.

Not in the same way or to the same measure, but they gave me things too: I've lived wonderful times with all of them. We must be grateful. And elegant. Because endings, if done well, can heighten the beauty of what took place; or, alternatively, they can cast it in shadows, to paraphrase Karmele Igartua.

How many times must I have muttered these lines through my teeth, as I cried and blew my nose: 'If I speak in the tongues of men or of angels, but do not have love, I am only a resounding gong or a clanging cymbal. If I have the gift of prophecy and can fathom all mysteries and all knowledge, and if I have a faith that can move mountains, but do not have love, I am nothing.' (The sacristan's grandchild obviously knows the epistle of the Corinthians well.) I'll never repeat them again.

I asked myself what was I missing, why didn't 'my men' love me wholly, since none of them has been able to take the measure of my chest (except with their hands). I had too much heart, not one bit was missing: there was always 300 grams of ground flesh on a polystyrene tray, on perpetual special offer.

But no. I've just come to realise that I was asking the wrong question. Now I know that no love will ever satisfy me: there is a type of loneliness that just never goes away.

They can be proud, those men: it's partly thanks to them that I am a poet.

But, what am I saying? I was always a poet. I've been writing compulsively since the moment I learnt to hold a pencil.

THE OCULAR PROSTHESIS, AN ARTISAN PIECE

As we all know, the term prosthesis is used to define the implements that are used to artificially substitute any missing body part.

Ocular prostheses are made out of methyl methacrylate because that's what's most advantageous in terms of weight and price. They are put in place after the enucleation, and their thickness oscillates between five and seven millimetres (what's required to emulate the eyeball's bulge).

It's recommendable to cast a mould of the cavity to create the prosthesis. For this purpose, alginic acid (a kind of white soup) is poured into the hollow, with the object of achieving the closest approximation to its shape. As soon as the liquid is solidified, the little ball is retrieved by means of a suction cup (it's uncomfortable, but not painful), and the lumps must be shaved off with a scalpel. Afterwards it must be carefully sanded down.

Once the surface is evened out, the pupil's centre is marked. It's usual to make several tests to imitate all of the elements too, always by comparing it to the real eye: its diameter and the colour of the iris; the sclera's tone; the quantity and look of the capillaries; and the size of the pupil. In any case, it's impossible to reproduce an eye identically.

Lastly, the previously painted mould is coated in a plastic resin and, *voilá*, to the hole. When you first wear it people notice something strange, it happens without fail. As soon as I sense their hesitance I say: 'It's the eye, it's a new one.'

It's the ocularist's responsibility to make their patient's face reflect wellbeing, at least to a degree. In the last thirty years four ocularists have looked after me, and not all of them were equally dextrous. I asked the last one to let me watch as he created my eye. I was very happy when I saw him paint my iris with a brown coloured Alpino pencil, rustle-rustle, focused and diligent, like an infant with good manual coordination handling his toy with the exact pressure, never ever painting outside the lines.

IN THE END

I spent hours looking for the sentences that would initiate this story. Bringing it to fruition has been like creating my own prosthesis. In the interim and until the end, words have been extremely hard to shape. And even though I've put a full stop in place, I am still dialoguing with what I wrote.

I could have gone over life with irony, like Elizabeth Bishop in her poem about the art of losing, and to joyfully say that I have learnt to master the art of losing more things, faster, because, in truth, *it's no disaster*. However, I found Olesia Nikolaeva's ambiguous bravery more fitting for the job at hand: *I walk around my losses like a mountaineer borders the edge of the ravine.*

You may not find the typical nuances of an intimate diary in my narrative. That was the risk, and it'll have consequences. Because, inevitably, I have become a character on these pages: even though this is me, it also isn't exactly me (accidentally and on purpose). Such are the advantages and limitations of self-imitation. Another *I* has emerged here, a slightly indomitable one that saw fit to escape my orders and shape into something of her own choosing (the same happened with M. and the rest), which I allowed.

I have constructed a biographical testimony that is as true as it is false, so thin is the dividing line between what happened and what I invented. I don't know if what I mean can be easily understood: a painting (whether it be a portrait, a landscape or a still life), even when it's a faithful copy of reality, is not reality. The glass eye is not made of glass either.

In the end, the glass eye is a peculiarity, just a physical defect to which I have awarded extraordinary importance impelled by literary interests. Let's not lie to ourselves.

Are you really going to believe everything I said?

I lost five or six kilos after the whole M. thing. Now, I'd say, with Colette, *give me a dozen such heartbreaks, if that would help me lose a couple of pounds.*

I've gotten over my anxiety of parking in parking garages.

Next summer I will wear a bikini, because showing my belly is a vindication that echoes the nakedness of this text (and all my bits of paper).

I have just taken on a modest commitment, although I won't be specific about what it entails.

I won't forget all these exploits, because they signal the beginning of a new era. What will follow afterwards? The wisdom of radical silence, perhaps: to turn writing into a *chemin privé* and fall silent.

I have read a lot in these two-and-a-half months (the quotes that pepper the text have helped me rise up). A special mention must go to Annie Ernaux's *Simple Passion.* That story taught me that some loves are non-refundable investments. I'll never posses the author's clairvoyance, but I feel forever linked to her because she sheltered me while I unravelled my chaos. I have also taken the liberty to copy, from J.M. Coetzee's *Summer,* the idea of adding footnotes and specifying the questions the text leaves unresolved.

This was my ambition, exactly: to offer a simple argument through precise sentences and logically assembled short paragraphs, backed up by the things I've lived and the propelling heartbeat of what's to come. The way in which events are portrayed, the depth of my observations, my effort to overcome shame and my literary style are all a reflection of my personality and my life's experiences. The breath of this text, in the end, stems from all of those things.

Vieux Bocau,
September 9ʰ⁻ November 22ⁿᵈ 2011

Chicago,
February 2017

'An exquisite novel by a great new talent.'
M. J. HYLAND

PIGEON
ALYS CONRAN

'...might have been authored by
Faulkner... pitch-perfect.'
OMAR SABBAGH,
NEW WELSH REVIEW

The Dylan Thomas Prize
Shortlisted
2017

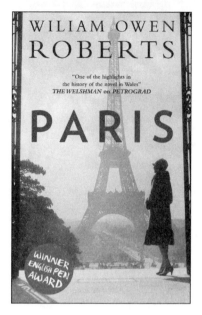

WILIAM OWEN
ROBERTS

"One of the highlights in
the history of the novel in Wales"
THE WELSHMAN on PETROGRAD

PARIS

WINNER
ENGLISH PEN
AWARD

PARTHIAN
A CARNIVAL OF VOICES

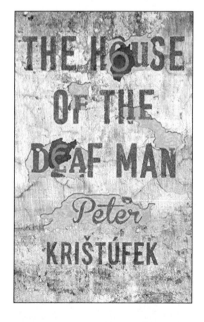

THE HOUSE
OF THE
DEAF MAN
Peter
KRIŠTÚFEK

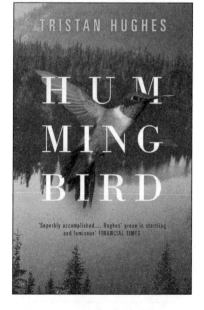

TRISTAN HUGHES

HUM
MING
BIRD

'Superbly accomplished... Hughes' prose is startling
and luminous' FINANCIAL TIMES

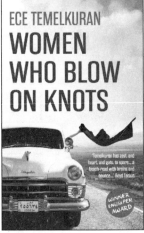

A Glass Eye
Miren Agur Meabe

Her Mother's Hands
Karmele Jaio